# The Enforcers

## BOOK 2 — ST. ANTONI - THE FORBIDDEN COLONY

# Gail Daley

# GAIL'S OTHER BOOKS

## SPACE COLONY JOURNALS
Options Of Survival
Destiny Rising
Tomorrows Legacy
The Interstellar Jewel Heist
The Designer People
Alien Trails
Quantum Light

## PORTAL WORLD TALES
## ST. ANTONI - THE FORBIDDEN COLONY
Warriors of St. Antoni
The Enforcers
The Gaslight Bandits
The Portal Lawman*
Cradle of Fire*

## MAGI OF RULARI
Spell Of The Magi
Magi Storm
Magi Flame*

## NON-FICTION
The Complete Modern Artist's Handbook

## PAMPHLETS
Introduction To The Internet #1
The Hard Stuff - Handbook #2
Art Show Basics - Handbook #3
Framing on a Budget - Handbook #4
Are You Making Money? - Handbook #5
*In the works. Release date to be announced.

GAIL DALEY

e-book ISBN: 9781393088974
Print ISBN- 9781393508908
Amazon ASIN:

For permission requests, write to the publisher, addressed "Attention: Permissions Coordinator," at the address below.

Gail Daley

5688 E Sussex Way

Fresno, CA 93727

www.gaildaley.com

Ordering Information: Quantity sales. Special discounts are available on quantity purchases by corporations, associations, and others. For details, contact the "Bulk Sales Department" at the address above.

Book Layout ©2017 BookDesignTemplates.com

## ABOUT THIS BOOK

*"This is novel about second chances."*

*"A fast-paced Sci-Fi novel of adventure, mystery and romance."*

*"A former assassin for hire plays a deadly game of cat and mouse with a serial killer on the Forbidden Colony planet of St. Antoni"*

Chloe was trained from a young age to be an assassin. Since her move to Junction City, she has been trying hard to reinvent herself as an investigator. But her first case has a huge complication: she finds Samuel Adams, the man she came to question, dead. He has a wicked knife sticking out of his groin. She didn't do it, but given her history, who will believe her? It looks as if her past is about to catch up with her.

Caleb Jones is a man with a violent past. After his family was destroyed in a city state war, he went to work at the only job he knew. As an Enforcer for the Marshals of the Federated City States of St. Antoni, he hunts killers. He came to Junction City looking for a serial killer. Instead he finds Chloe. Is she the killer he's looking for or the woman who can replace everything he lost?

## Table of Contents

# PROLOGUE

THE STOREKEEPER was nervous. His chest felt tight and he had trouble catching his breath. Someone was watching him; he could feel it, but he hadn't found the watcher, but he thought he knew who was paying him; it had been a mistake to dally with such a dangerous man's wife, but the danger had added a spice to his sexual excitement. He poured another glass of expensive Earth whiskey and downed it hastily. The bottle was almost empty. He would need to order another from the Portal Runner. Hell, why not order a case? He had money now.

There was a sound from the back of the storeroom. His wife? No, she was asleep upstairs, zonked out on that sleeping potion she had taken.

A sudden cramp caused him to double over. He looked at the whisky bottle in sudden suspicion. His last thought as he slid down the counter to the floor was, he had been poisoned!

The killer stood in the doorway to the storage room and watched dispassionately as Adams puked up the Whiskey he had just drunk. He had been paid to kill the storekeeper in a certain way. Poisoning the man wasn't in his instructions and he had already been paid. He shrugged, and rolled Adams over with his foot. He took

the knife he had taken from the kitchen and drove it into the body several times, leaving it sticking out of the man's groin. He would have preferred to use one of his own knives, but he wouldn't have left it behind as he had been instructed.

## WHITE IN THE MOON

CHLOE STOOD on the deck of the steamer Sally Sue watching River Crossing slide off into the distance. As they pulled away from the hustle and bustle of the busy waterfront, the noise of the town dropped away. Instead there was the sound of the fifty or sixty passengers and crew and the muted splash of water falling as it was pulled through the paddlewheel driven by a mighty bluestone steam engine.

Although not born on St. Antoni (her mother had escaped Earth with her when she had been only a few months old), Chloe had grown to womanhood on the forbidden colony. Had she been transported back to earth she would have found its people and technology strange and alien. To Chloe, there was nothing strange in the juxtaposition of St. Antoni's mixed primitive and modern technology. It was primitive by earth standards; without Earth's powerful manufacturing base to maintain and create advanced technology, the colony had been forced to fall back on more primitive means to maintain their standard of living. Instead of gas-powered transportation, they domesticated native animals to ride and to pull plows or carriages. As an alternative to using coal to power steam engines, they used a native mineral; bluestones. Bluestones were unique to St. Antoni; when water was poured on them, they burst into flame and continued to produce heat until the mineral was absorbed by the water.

Good fortune had shone on the settlers of St. Antoni when they first snuck through the illicit portal. They found a world that closely resembled Earth in the Pleistocene epoch. Settlers using other illicit gates weren't always so lucky: some of them found themselves stranded on rocky wastelands whose soil lacked the nutrients to maintain life or a water covered planet with little or no land to grow crops.

St. Antoni possessed a yellow sun only a little darker than the one that shone on Earth. The constellations overhead might be new and strange, but the sun looked down on blue seas, lush grass covered land masses with dense forests, high snowy mountains, and hot dry deserts. Large rivers and small streams threaded the continents. Plants and animals were genetically close enough to those on Earth to support human life, and St. Antoni's temperature range made living there bearable for humans.

St. Antoni was still wild and unexplored except for a few roads connecting isolated farms and ranches to towns and the railroads directly connecting the City States to each other. However the illegal portal from Earth in Gateway City had been open for several hundred years, and in that time the citizens of St. Antoni had established seven City States whose loosely connected governments cooperated with each other to keep anarchy from thriving.

Back on Earth, daring Portal Runners dodged police and military to bring in a steady trickle of new settlers and other items highly valued on a planet without its own technological resources.

The only other means of getting from place to place was by using the rivers. Like others of her kind, the Sally Sue, the riverboat Chloe and her companions had booked passage on, regularly traversed the Black River to and from Junction City and the coast. She was a large flat-bottomed boat; the wheelhouse stuck up in the middle of the boat. Passenger cabins took up the next two decks below it, with a cargo hold at the bottom of the boat. Half of Sally Sue's large upper deck was taken up by walled corrals holding livestock. A portion of the other half was used by travelers who couldn't afford the price of a cabin. During the day these passengers lounged on the luggage they had brought, passing the time by playing cards and

other games of chance.

The Riverboats plying the Black River usually traveled during daylight hours and dropped anchor overnight. Even with a good navigator, sand bars and boulders made it too dangerous to travel at night on a river. During the day it was possible to see low water just below the surface or obstacles sticking up out of the water. If she hit them going at any speed it might wreck the steamer.

At night deck passengers would lay out bedrolls and sleep in the open air. Cabins for the more affluent passengers were located on the deck opposite the corrals. Chloe and her companions, her godmother Giselle and her best friend and maid Lizette, had been fortunate to secure a cabin, but they would be sharing it with another family. Henry had taken one of the cots in the bunkroom reserved for single men.

Chloe was slight, with curling dark hair worn in a braid wound around the crown of her head. A wide brimmed straw hat trimmed with feathers shaded the creamy skin of her heart shaped face. Her Large dark eyes were set above a short, straight nose and her generous naturally red lips offset her determined chin.

Despite technological advances such as steam engines and refrigerators to keep food from spoiling, St. Antoni was a frontier society. Chloe had turned twenty this month, an age when many girls her age were married. Chloe's marital status didn't concern her much; unlike many women she didn't need to secure a husband to support her. Thanks to her mother's tutoring, Chloe had a unique skill set that would always ensure she could feed and clothe herself. While those skills gave her independence, she had never met a man she thought could accept the unusual profession for which she had been trained. What man wanted to marry a woman who knew a thousand ways to kill him and not get caught? It wasn't as if she was resigned to being single the rest of her life; like any girl her age she dreamed of falling in love. Her mother had found her true love. Chloe kept hoping the dream could become real for her as well.

Although she wasn't ashamed of how her mother had supported them and was grateful her skills gave her the ability to support herself, Chloe always needed to force herself to kill the target. When her Godmother Giselle St. Vyr offered Chloe the opportunity to re-invent herself as an investigator, she grabbed it eagerly. Junction City was going to be her fresh start.

On Earth, Chloe's mother Angela had

been good at her job. Angela had been schooled as a spy and an assassin by a government agency. When she made the mistake of falling in love with the man she was assigned to kill, her agency turned on her. She and Charles DeMille fled, taking false identities and hiding underground. When Angela discovered she was going to have a child, she was both elated and terrified. Nine months later she gave birth to a girl and named her Chloe. Angela had heard about a man who offered passage through one of the illegal gates to another world--for a price. She and Charles made the decision to escape from Earth to St. Antoni where they hoped to make a fresh start.

Unfortunately they didn't get away unscathed; the organization found them the night they were to go through the portal. Charles sent Angela ahead with a promise to follow them after he had laid a false trail. He made her promise she would go through the gate without him if he didn't arrive in time. "I'll follow you," he said. "Wait for me."

Angela never saw her love again, and life on St. Antoni was hard for a single woman with a baby. Like many before her, Angela soon realized that on St. Antoni women as well as men were expected to be able to protect, feed and clothe themselves on their own. Here, a woman had to be tough enough to do those things or find a man to do it for her. Since Angela still had some hope her husband might make it through the Portal, she took steps to protect herself and her three-month old baby.

She wasn't without resources. She had brought ten thousand dollars in paper bills with her when she fled through the portal. The paper money might be useless on St. Antoni, but it could be used by Portal Runners returning to Earth to purchase items needed in a society with few technological resources. Angela had approached the leader of the Women's Circle for help.

Like Angela, Giselle had been left alone on St. Antoni with a child to raise soon after she had arrived. She and a few other women banded together to help each other, developing the Women's Circle in the process. When she met Angela, Giselle had been an attractive woman in her forties, and she had still possessed the trim figure that drew men's eyes. An immediate friendship had blossomed between the two women, and Giselle became Chloe's godmother.

Giselle understood Angela's situation all too well; after her arrival on St. Antoni, her husband had been murdered. To

support herself and her son, she had done a variety of things; she had once been a successful Portal Runner, told fortunes with tarot cards, and sold jewelry she made from gems. She now lived in Copper City and sold rare gemstones and herbal medicines. She wasn't often in Gateway City anymore, and another woman now ran the Women's Circle there, but she made yearly tours of each of the cities to check on the operations of what she had founded. Unsure what to do about Angela, the local head of the Women's Circle had sent her to Giselle.

"I can pay," Angela said when she made her request to change her Earth money for the coins and gems used on St. Antoni as currency.

Giselle had gestured to the pile of bills on the table before her. "It's true that one of the Portal Runners might be able to use this money back on Earth to buy items ordered, but if the bills are marked someone might be watching for them. That would draw unwanted attention to the Runner using them."

"They aren't marked," Angela had said. "I drew it from our hidden accounts just before we left. But if you think it's too dangerous to use, I can pay in kind."

"With what?"

Angela took a deep breath. "Who do you

want killed?"

Ostensibly the Circle existed to give help to women in the area who needed it, supplying them with food, medicines and clothing. Unknown to all but a few leaders, it sometimes removed threats as well. So Angela became an agent of the Women's Circle. Having no one to leave her baby with when she took an assignment, Angela took Chloe with her wherever she went. As soon as Chloe was old enough, she had begun to teach her daughter the tricks of her trade.

Angela had done her best to ensure that Chloe could support herself by teaching her daughter the only trade she knew, and Chloe had continued to ply it after Angela had died on an assignment in Azure City. When her mother had been killed on that job, fourteen-year-old Chloe had finished the contract. She had been earning her living ever since as a paid assassin. Unfortunately, the local sheriff in Azure City had become suspicious, so Marie Nguyn, the local leader of the Woman's Circle had sent Chloe to Giselle in Kenefic.

Giselle had taken Chloe aside soon after she arrived in River Crossing to speak about her career choices.

"Do you like what you are doing for the Circle?" she had asked.

Chloe bit her lip. "It's what my mother did, what I'm trained for," she replied.

"That isn't what I asked." Giselle had said mildly. "I asked you if you liked it."

Chloe had thought about sickening feeling of her knife sliding into the target's body and shuddered inwardly. "No, I don't," she replied. "But what else can I do?"

"I thought you might use your skills to become an investigator," Giselle had said calmly. "While you are building up your clientele, you can earn a living by selling cosmetics and healing potions."

"The only potions I actually know how to make are poisons," Chloe pointed out.

"I suspected as much. As it happens, I know a great deal about creating cosmetics and healing potions. If you want to learn, I can teach you."

"Thank you," Chloe had said, blinking back tears. "I would like to learn."

Chloe's thoughts returned to the present and she turned her head when she heard Giselle's light footsteps behind her on the deck.

"Henry made sure our trunks are in our room," Giselle said, joining her at the rail. "And I left Lizette there with the bags. Unfortunately, we don't have it to ourselves. We are sharing with a woman and her daughters, a Mrs. Dominique."

"Is she the one who was ranting at the crew when we boarded?"

Giselle made a face. "Yes, I believe so. The four girls seem quiet and well behaved though. The two older girls are about your age."

Chloe eyed her. "Does that mean you want me to befriend them?"

"Not unless you want to. I just thought someone to talk to besides me and Lizette might make the journey pass faster."

"Alright."

Although Chloe found the Dominique girls pleasant company, she soon realized she had little in common with Lila, the oldest girl, whose life seemed centered around finding a husband. Lila had soft, dark hair, blue eyes, pretty features and a timid disposition. Francis, the second oldest daughter was different. The family resemblance was there; Francis too had dark hair and blue eyes, but her tall, spare figure lacked the pleasing shape of her elder sister. Her looks were striking rather than pretty; she possessed cut-glass cheekbones, a firm mouth and intelligent eyes. Francis also had a lively wit and a sharp tongue which she was careful how she exercised around her mother. She was a reader and as she and Chloe shared views on books and life, they

found a lot in common. Francis was possessed of an independent streak lacking in her sister. The next oldest daughter, Hetty was about thirteen and her sister Sydney about ten. Both the younger girls had the family dark hair and blue eyes.

Francis was puzzled by her mother's tolerance of her developing friendship with Chloe DeMille. As a rule Cora Dominique kept her daughters close, stringently supervising any friendships that came their way, and discouraging any that might lead to association with what Cora considered the lower classes. True, Chloe and her mentor Giselle St. Vyr seemed to have connections with the upper strata of Junction City, but both women had an independent attitude which Cora didn't want rubbing off on her daughters.

Cora had homeschooled the girls, as much to discourage them making friends with unsuitable classmates, as to ensure that despite their nomadic lifestyle the girls were well fitted for the life she intended them to lead. Francis and Lila could embroider delicate designs, paint pretty pictures, run a house, plan a party and in short do anything expected of the wife of a wealthy man. Despite her mother's insistence they make wealthy marriages, the family was never short of money. As she grew older, Francis had wondered more than once if her father did something on the side besides bookkeeping to account for the additional money she recorded as the family bookkeeper. Whatever it was, she was sure if it wasn't illegal, it probably skirted it. It would account for the frequent moves from city to city and her mother's stringent supervision of any friendships the girls tried to make.

During their last days in Azure City, Cora had been increasingly desperate to marry off her daughters. When the letter from their father ordering them to come to Junction City had arrived, it had obviously angered her, but she had obeyed it. Cora always submitted to their father's orders. Having grown up with her parent's behavior, it didn't occur to Francis how odd the relationship was. On the surface Cora Dominique was the ruler of her family. In public, she might nag and criticize her husband, but in private she obeyed him implicitly.

Although Cora allowed Francis to peruse local libraries and bookstores, she always cautioned her not to broadcast her wide-ranging interests. "Most men don't want an intellectual for a wife," she had cautioned. "Novels are an acceptable interest for a lady, so confine any discussions of books you've read to them."

Whatever her mother's reasons for allowing it, Francis was enjoying making her first real friend in Chloe, partly because Chloe shared her interest in subjects like history and science as well as in novels. She had ignored her mother's ban on speaking of those subjects to Chloe and the pair passed the time with many a lively discussion, occasionally joined by the younger girls. Hetty usually took no part in the debates but listened avidly. Sydney preferred to draw in her sketchbook.

The trip upriver took five days. Junction City was located at the headwaters of three rivers, the Sanguine, Thunderfalls Run and Whispering Waters. It was also the base where the new railroad lines connecting the City States met.

It was the furthest inland settlement on St. Antoni. In the beginning, the new immigrants had stayed close to the Portal, but colonists had long since migrated to the coastal areas where the climate was cooler, the soil fertile and the fishing plentiful. Junction City sat at the northern edge of the territory claimed by the City State of Kenefic. Beyond it, to the north and across it to the west lay terra incognita. Even though it was now summer, high mountains to the north and west showed snowy peaks.

On the fifth morning, when they had docked at the busy river port Chloe had awakened to a cacophony of sound. Junction city was a busy place. During any given day it was common to see more than a hundred steamboats lining the cobblestone levees to unload cargo and passengers.

A wooden gangplank allowed the Sally Sue's passengers and their luggage to debark onto the long wooden wharf running the length of the town waterfront. An assortment of rickshaws and carriages crowded into the street around the end of every gangplank where a boat had docked. The air resounded with yells and curses as dockmen and drivers tried to gain access to the departing passengers and cargoes.

Across from the wharf were warehouses where cargo could be stored. Narrow streets sprawled through the warehouse district to more affluent areas. Along these streets, eating houses and saloons sat cheek by jowl with places where inexpensive rooms could be rented by the day or the week.

Further away from the Wharf area was the Red Rock District where the more expensive houses and hotels were frequented by the rich and newly rich of the town. The further from the docks, the more expensive the hotel rooms, Giselle had told Chloe.

"When I came here with Iris and Jeanne we stayed in a hotel. Since we will be here longer this time, I asked my friend Amy Wong to make arrangements for us to rent a house."

"A house means nosy servants," Chloe had reminded her.

"I trust Amy," Giselle had said. "She will have hired trustworthy people to work there. Even if they are curious about our doings, they won't talk about it. She wrote me the house is in a quiet neighborhood and has an attached stable behind it for the tricorns as well."

When the first colonists arrived on St. Antoni it was immediately obvious that they needed a source of transportation, Since they had left behind motorized cars and trucks an alternative method was needed that didn't require factories to make or ran on gas and oil that needed refineries to use. Inspiration came from history. Man had domesticated horses for centuries. The tricorns who ranged the valleys and plains of the new world in large herds, made an admirable substitute. Tricorns resembled large horses with two slim horns poking out of a broad forehead and a short, blunt horn just above their nostrils. Tricorns came with a variety of colors but the most common was red and black striped coats. The stripes, like

those of zebras on Earth's savannah's, enabled the wild tricorn herds to blend in with the grasses found on much of St. Antoni's prairie lands. Once tamed to man's use, the settlers rode the tricorns and used them to pull plows or other forms of transportation much the way their ancestors on Earth had used horses and oxen.

Chloe had left her own gruella tricorn back at Rancho De Oro with Bethany who bred and trained racing tricorns. The mare was in foal and she didn't want to chance the river voyage with her. Also, Marie Nguyn had told her the Sheriff in Azure City had been questioning stablemen there about a Tricorn that looked like hers. It was better for the mare to remain in Bethany St. Vyr's stable where her presence would go unremarked.

They had brought riding animals from the ranch with them. During the trip upriver, the animals had stayed on deck with other livestock also being transported.

A tall thin man in stableman's clothes came up the gangplank. He glanced around until he spotted Giselle, Lizette and Chloe standing by the pile of luggage Giselle had deemed necessary to bring with them.

"Mrs. St. Vyr?" he asked, doffing his

hat.

"Yes, I'm Giselle St. Vyre," she answered.

"I'm Terry. Joe sent me. I'm to take you and your luggage to the new house. Is this it?" he asked, pointing at the mound of trunks and bags.

"Yes. We also have four riding mounts. Henry is seeing to them."

"Which one is Henry?" the man asked, gesturing at the crowd around the animal enclosures.

"That's him," she pointed at Henry, "He's the man in the grey shirt with the red and white tricorns."

"Excuse me, a moment, Mrs. St. Vyr," Terry said. He moved over to Henry.

"Your Amy appears to be efficient," Chloe remarked. "Is Joe her husband?"

"Yes, they are old friends. Uh-oh, here comes Mrs. Dominique. I wonder what she wants."

Cora Dominique was a tall blowsy woman with graying hair. She was trailed by her four pretty daughters and her husband Larry, a thin man with a patch of bald pate, who had come aboard to meet them. He appeared to be remonstrating with her.

"Are you leaving the ship?" Cora asked Giselle.

"Yes, we've taken a house here," Giselle answered.

"The prices they want for transporting our bags is simply outrageous. I noticed you were met by that man with a wagon. Could you take us to our rooming house?"

"Cora that is an imposition," her husband whispered.

"Nonsense Larry!" Cora's voice boomed. "I'm sure Giselle won't mind, will you dear?"

Chloe, who had glanced at Larry Dominique when he remonstrated with his wife, was startled when she saw the murderous rage in his eyes as his wife dismissed his complaint, However, the flash was gone so fast, she thought she must have been mistaken.

"Where are you staying?" Giselle asked her.

"Not one of these places around the docks," Cora said with disdain. "I have daughters. I don't want them exposed to this riffraff. We might no longer have money, but we can do better, I'm sure."

"Did you make reservations?" Giselle asked.

"No, but I'm sure we can find something. Since you have a house, perhaps we could stay with you until we get settled?"

"No, I'm sorry but the house we rented is much too small to accommodate all of you as well as ourselves. Why don't I ask

Terry to find you transport to the Hotel Royale? I'm sure they can put you up there until you find something that suits you better."

"Those prices are too high," Cora protested.

"I'll take care of the transport charges," Giselle assured her, and moved over to where Henry and Terry were discussing unloading the Tricorns.

"I'm sorry," Lila, Cora's oldest daughter, whispered. "Mother can be pushy."

"Mother's up to her old tricks, I see," Francis observed. "We aren't as poor as she makes out. She just doesn't like to spend money."

Lizette snorted rudely, rolling her eyes.

Chloe grinned at her. "Don't let it worry you. Giselle can handle her. Perhaps you and I can get together after we've all settled in. I'll send our direction to the Hotel."

Giselle had arrived back with Terry in tow.

"Come with me," he told the Dominique's. "I think I have a driver that will suit you. Is that your stuff?" he pointed at another large pile of luggage.

"Yes," Larry Dominique answered.

Terry gestured, and two of the long

shoremen waiting on the deck gathered up the bags and followed him down the gangplank.

Chloe watched them depart. "That was slick," she told Giselle. "You aren't intending to pay for their transport, are you?"

"You bet I am," Giselle retorted. "Anything is better than having to endure that woman's company. Besides, I don't want her to have our address."

Chloe looked guilty. "I already told Francis I would send it to her."

"Don't you worry about that Miss Chloe," Lizette, Giselle's longtime maid and companion said. "This one's got a lot to learn, but she has possibilities," she informed Giselle, who snorted in reply.

# THE ENFORCER

A MONTH before Chloe and Giselle decided to make the trip upriver to Junction City, Caleb Jones stood in front of the office of the Consolidated City State Law Enforcement Bureau in Gateway City. Caleb was a man of medium height, with the dark, harshly cut features that marked the men of his family. He moved with an economy of movement characteristic of men who led outdoor lives.

He directed the three massive canines accompanying him to lie down in the shade between the hitching rail and the boardwalk to wait for him. The dogs, like many of the colonists had ancestors born on Earth. They showed their Rottweiler bloodlines in their large, muscular bodies and powerful jaws. The strain had been mixed with Collie breeds to add intelligence and they had taken their multicolored fur from that breed.

Gateway City, St. Antoni's oldest settlement, rested on the edge of a prairie of buttery grass stretching halfway across the continent. Behind it were low rolling hills that gradually rose into mountains. The foothills were split by a long valley extending south to the ocean.

The gateway portal, a stone edifice

tall and wide enough to drive several wagons through could be seen for several miles. The colonists hadn't built the arch. It had been there when the first men walked through the gate to St. Antoni and no one knew its origins. Once a week, the Portal regularly disgorged travelers making the one-way trip from Earth to St. Antoni. Only the Portal Runners made the dangerous journey back to earth to smuggle needed items and escaping earth citizens to St. Antoni. The Runners earned a livelihood by smuggling in goods and people from Earth. The Portal settlement act made it against the law to open, travel to or return from an unsanctioned Portal. Portal Running was dangerous work. The penalty for violating the act was imprisonment, a hefty fine and sometimes the death penalty was imposed. It was also lucrative; Runners who risked imprisonment and sometimes their lives to return to Earth and bring back desperately needed items for the colony could get rich if they were willing to take the risks.

A ramshackle camp of tents and wooden shacks for temporary residents and people recently arrived spread out around the Arch portal. A few enterprising St. Antonians had erected several rows of bunkhouses made of clay bricks, divided into rooms that could be rented out to newcomers if they could pay. There were bathing rooms as well (also for a price). At the edge of the camp were businesses where the newly arrived could change Earth money for coins minted on St. Antoni and buy food and other items needed for survival. The money was traded to the Portal Runners who used it on return trips to Earth.

Having been open for two hundred years, Gateway City showed some signs of civilization. Older mansions owned by affluent residents graced the wooded hills surrounding the edge of the town on one side. The mansions were supplanted in their turn by homes and businesses owned by middle class residents. The town and its neatly kept streets were lined with stores, offices, cafes, boarding houses and respectable saloons. Dividing the Camp from the town was a large stone building that housed Peacekeepers employed by the Bertelli family to ensure order in the city. Pedro Bertelli, Gateway City's mayor, had given orders to the Peacekeepers to make sure the new emigrants weren't robbed or murdered if it could be avoided. He knew if this became common practice it would lead to revolt; it was during such a rebellion that the Bertelli's had taken Gateway City away from the Tresoni's who had previously run it.

Out toward the edge of town on the other side of the new railroad depot were less savory enterprises such as gambling dens, pleasure houses, bars, bunkhouses where beds were rented by the day and a few eating places made their homes.

The eight City states established since St. Antoni was discovered, occupied a small portion of one of the northern continents; most of them along the southern coast. Each City state claimed a separate territory. These City states and the adjoining smaller towns were controlled by powerful families or groups. Outlying ranches and mines outside the immediate borders of the settlements were held together by guns and guts. But the St. Antonians new civilization had a flaw: a man or woman could commit crimes in one City state, flee to another and be safe from pursuit. The new citizens of St. Antoni found this intolerable. However, none of the rulers of a city state wanted armed groups invading their territory to capture outlaws, so a compromise was reached. They created the Enforcers: an elite law enforcement bureau commissioned to pursue lawbreakers across the borders. An Enforcer was obliged to notify local law enforcement of their presence in an area and were entitled to cooperation from local lawmen. Efforts were made to return captured outlaws to the City State where a crime had been committed, but an Enforcer could use deadly force if the outlaw proved uncooperative.

Caleb Jones was mostly uninterested in the historical settlement of St. Antoni or what life had been like on Earth . He was a fourth-generation emigrant and a man who concerned himself foremost with day-to-day survival. After his family had lost Copper City to the Smiths, he had joined the Bureau. He was here at the Gateway office of the branch of the Consolidated City State Law Enforcement Bureau because he had been recalled from an assignment to find a hired killer.

The office didn't look like much; It was on a side street and occupied the second floor over a tailor's shop. It consisted of two public rooms; a reception area where visitors stated their business and the inner office of the man who controlled the bureau. Visitors waited to be seen on uncomfortable wooden chairs. The second room held the office occupied by the current head of the bureau: a retired Enforcer named Jorge Rodriguez. Rodriguez was of Hispanic descent, with dark hair going grey, and a once hard body going soft from inaction. There was nothing soft about his mind, however.

The office held a battered desk and file cabinet that had both seen better days and a single wooden chair for visitors, bare of any kind of cushion. In one corner, next to the door was am equally battered coat tree sitting in a metal bucket that held umbrellas when it rained. A bulletin board with various paper notices tacked on it graced a wall across from Jorge's desk.

Jorge was ostensibly Caleb's boss. This morning he regarded the man across from him over his steepled fingers. Outwardly Jorge was the picture of calm composure. Inwardly, he was conscious of a faint unease and it annoyed him. There was no reason for it; he was certainly in no danger from his most efficient Enforcer.

However, Caleb Jones nearly always had that effect on those around him. He was a medium built man in a faded blue shirt and grey pants. His somber grey eyes regarded Jorge out of a sharp featured weather-beaten face, tanned brown by exposure to St. Antoni's sun. A thin scar along his face ran from his hairline to his jaw. The scar was a reminder of a knife fight.

A five-pointed metal badge with the initials CCSE was pinned to his shirt. The initials stood for Consolidated City States Enforcement. A pistol in a holster belt with loops for shells hung around his

waist. When he had entered the room, Caleb had hung his leather hat on the hat rack over the coat tree and placed his rifle butt down in the bucket.

"You're late. I expected you yesterday," Jorge said.

"I was delayed in Azure City," Caleb replied. "I had to drop everything in the Sheriff's lap to come here."

"I know. Sorry about that, but Azure isn't the only city with a series of killings. Junction City has requested someone with experience come there to see if any connection between the murders can be found."

"What about that rich farmer and that rancher from Kenefic the Azure sheriff thinks were paid killings?"

Jorge shrugged. "I can assign someone else to that. Didn't you say you thought the killer had left Azure City?"

"I do. I also think this is a person who will keep killing unless we stop him."

Jorge sighed. Jones could stick to a task like a burr on a tricorn. "You're good, maybe the best investigator I've got. But until we can get something to back up the theory this is a contract killer, we need to do some routine checking. I've assigned Leroy Corks to go through the back records in Azure City to look for similar killings. You can do the same while you are in Junction City."

"Do you think they are connected?" Caleb asked.

"What I think is I need more people with your experience in making connections between crimes. As a matter of fact, I need to you to meet a possible recruit and assess her abilities."

Jones eyed him warily. "Her?" he asked cautiously.

"That's right, it's a female," Jorge said. "We have only a few female investigators, and there are some situations where that is a real handicap, especially if we are looking at a crime in upper social circles."

"I was under the impression the Bureau already had an investigator working in Junction City," Caleb said.

"Yes, we do, but he's working deep undercover. I can't risk exposing him until he's finished his investigation."

"Why me?" Jones asked.

"Because I need someone to do the evaluation who can also move in those social circles," Jorge told him.

He took out a letter and handed it to Caleb. "This is the recommendation. The woman's name is Chloe DeMille."

Caleb frowned as he read through the letter. "Who is this Giselle St. Vyr who is recommending her?"

"She is a friend of my wife's. She asked Juanita to pass on the request."

"Is this woman qualified to make a recommendation for an investigator?"

"Yes," Jorge replied. He made no other explanation.

Knowing his boss had said all he was going to about Giselle St. Vyr, Caleb sighed. "Where do I find her?"

"I believe Chloe DeMille and Mrs. St. Vyr are in Junction City. You can catch a train and be there in three days."

Jones frowned. "DeMille, where have I heard that name before?"

"A woman name Angela DeMille occasionally did some work for the Bertelli family here in Gateway. I believe this woman Chloe is her daughter."

Caleb kept his inevitable reflections to himself. The Bertelli's ruled Gateway City with an iron hand. If the DeMille woman had worked for them, there was no telling what type of work she had done. He wasn't foolish enough to ask; the Bertelli's, like most of the families who ruled the City States took a dim view of too much curiosity about their private affairs.

Jorge hesitated, tapping his fingers on the desk, unsure how he wanted to approach the next topic. "How much do you know about the Bureau's future plans?"

"I don't pay much attention to politics anymore. You know that," Caleb replied.

"Eventually, the Bureau wants to have a satellite office in every City State. Junction City is the next largest settlement next to Gateway. I need a man who can deal with all layers of society to head it. Are you interested?"

The question took Caleb completely by surprise. Ever since he had brought Jake Smith to justice for Julia's murder, he had been aware of a vaguely unsettled feeling. The immediate spark of sexual interest jolted him.

"How much autonomy would I have?"

Jorge smiled. The fish had taken the bait. "As much as I have here," he said.

When he stepped out of the building several minutes later, Caleb stopped and took stock of his surroundings. It was an old habit and it had kept him alive on more than one occasion.

He made a clucking sound and the three canines joined him on the wooden sidewalk. They also stopped and looked over the street. The devoted animals, Cernunnos, Athena and Aphrodite, were the only things he had taken with him when he shook the dust of Copper City off his boots.

When he left Copper City for the last time, he had stopped at the gravesite of his baby sister Julia. He had looked down

at the mound of rocks with its marble headstone and told her, "I'll get him for you, I promise."

Julia had been barely fifteen when she died. Murdered by Jake Smith who had fled the city when he realized his brother Frank, the new head of the Smith family, wouldn't protect him from the consequences of his crime. The only thing that prevented Caleb from immediately hunting Jake down to avenge Julia's death had been Jake's flight. Caleb had been too busy trying to defend the family to chase after him immediately.

Julia's rape and murder had brought the hostilities between the two clans to a head. It had sparked a seven-month war that eventually led to the Jones Family losing control of Copper City.

Caleb and the three hounds had left the city when he realized that the only way to save the rest of the family was to run. The Jones clan had scattered to the four winds. Unlike Smith, however, Caleb had done something productive after the truce was declared; he had joined the Enforcers, the elite law enforcement arm of the Joint City States. His new job protected him from having a bounty on his head. As it appeared the Smiths were willing to abide by the truce, he did his job and waited with a deadly patience for a lead on Jacob

Smith's whereabouts.

Three months ago, Caleb's patience had been rewarded. A madam in River Crossing had run afoul of Smith, now living under the name of Jacob Lutz. Smith was making a fortune foreclosing on hapless miners and farmers. When Smith had tried to fight being taken in for judgement, Caleb hadn't shed any tears over his death.

"Well, boys and girls," Caleb said to his three faithful companions, who cocked their ears attentively, "It looks like a train ride is in our future."

By the end of the month he found himself in the local Sheriff's Office. Trace Melody was around forty, with salt and pepper hair and a tough, wiry body. He greeted Caleb with a smile and a handshake.

"Welcome to Junction City, Enforcer Jones. You got here fast. I wasn't expecting you until the end of the week."

"I was between assignments," Caleb said. "I understand you're have a bunch of murdered whores on your hands."

"Yes, the latest one is probably still on the coroner's examination table. Let's go see if we can catch him before he goes home."

Caleb looked down at the naked body of the young woman lying on the table in the morgue. She had been washed off, but

numerous shallow cuts marked her breasts and thighs, and she was missing the ring finger on her left hand. Dr. Sanderson, the coroner, had just been explaining that she had died from multiple stab wounds.

"She's the latest victim?" Caleb asked Sheriff Melody, who was avoiding allowing his eyes to drop to the body.

"Yes," Melody said. "Thank you Doctor for sharing your findings with us."

Melody moved toward the door obviously glad to get out of the depressing room.

"We've had four like this so far. No clues at the crime scenes, just a lot of blood."

They crossed the street to the Sheriff's office. Once there, Melody handed Caleb several files. "These are the others."

Caleb opened the first file and looked up in surprise. "You had the scene photographed?"

"I did; we aren't entirely backward here. A few months ago, a young man came in and offered his services photographing crime scenes. It seemed like a good idea. Of course he isn't full time, I can't afford to keep him on salary."

"What does he do in the meantime?" Caleb asked, spreading the photos out in a line on the desk. They were black and white and surprisingly clear. "I'd say you were fortunate to get his services. These are some of the best I've ever seen for this kind of work."

He carefully went through the files, noting similarities and differences between each murder. The women were all in their twenties or thirties, the pitiless camera lens revealed the hard life they had been leading.

"Did you find any connection between the girls?" he asked Melody.

Melody shook his head. "Just that they were all working girls. They didn't even belong to the same pimp." He rose and went to the bluestone stove in the corner and lifted a metal coffee pot. "Want some?" he asked.

"No thanks," Caleb said.

Melody sat back down. "Some girls will work in a group or out of a house. These girls all worked alone and usually serviced the client in their own rooms."

"So the killer picked them because they were vulnerable."

"Looks that way."

Caleb had been looking through the files again. "I see that almost no one in the area admitted to hearing anything. Are they scared to talk or just indifferent?"

"Both, probably. I had my deputies ask around to see if anyone had seen any strangers watching the girls, but so far no luck."

One of the deputies, a tall thin young man with a bobbing Adams Apple looked in the door. "Boss there's a kid out here says there's a dead man in Adams Mercantile," he said.

"Thanks Sims. Dr. Sanderson should still be in his office and see if you can find that photographer—what's his name? Doimer and send them along. Want to come with me?" he asked Caleb.

"Sure," Caleb agreed.

Melody eyed the three huge canines waiting with Caleb's tricorns. "They friendly?"

"If I tell them to be," Caleb answered. "Okay to leave the packhorse here?"

"Sure. I'll tell one of my men to put him in the police stable."

## A DISMAL SHEEN

A WEEK EARLIER, Chloe had found herself waiting to disembark from the steamship that had brought her to Junction City. The wagon Joe Wang had sent to the boat docks to pick up Giselle's party was large enough to hold the three women and all their luggage. A pair of well-muscled tricorns waited placidly while their luggage was loaded. Henry threw Chloe, Lizette, and Giselle's saddles on top of the luggage and mounted his own tricorn, intending to lead the other animals through the town.

"All set?" Terry asked as he swung into the driver's seat.

"Yes," Chloe said. "Did you get the Dominique's a wagon to take their stuff?"

He grinned at her. "I did. The missus wasn't too pleased with it, but when I told her it had already been paid for, she got on board without too much fuss."

He clucked to the tricorns and they pulled away from the gangplank. It was obvious Terry was experienced at threading a way through traffic. He easily avoided getting tangled in a dispute between two cabs who had managed to get their wheels stuck together.

The house he took them to was in a quiet neighborhood shaded by tall broadleaf trees. It was enclosed by a six-foot high stone wall. Access was through a gate. A small structure adjacent to the gate provided shelter for a gatekeeper. A young boy opened the wrought iron gate when he saw the wagon approaching, closing it behind Henry and the Tricorns as Terry drove the wagon around the circular drive to stop in front of the wide terraced steps.

The house was stone on the bottom story with a timbered upper. In the rear was a stable and a vegetable garden. On St. Antoni the trees shading the yard weren't ornamental. They had been planted with fruits and nuts which could be harvested and stored for the winter or sold to less fortunate neighbors.

On the other side of the house, far enough away to be safe if they got wet and caught fire, was the standard Bluestone enclosure. Racks of Bluestones to power a steam generator were stored on layers of frames under a roof supported by long poles. This was done to prevent them from gathering moisture and catching on fire. Bluestones had been discovered by accident soon after the first colonists arrived. A man spilled some water on a pile of them and they burst into flame. His partner, an engineer, experimented with adapting the chemical reaction from the mixture of

stones and water to create enough heat to run a steam engine. The first steam generators had been made from parts smuggled in from Earth , but the engineer and his partner soon got rich making their own generators with parts made from a home-made alloy of iron, carbon, copper and tin.

"This is a small house?" Chloe asked incredously.

"You don't like it?" Terry asked anxiously.

"Oh, we like it," Giselle assured him. "It's beautiful. Amy did a splendid job choosing it."

A middle-aged woman met them at the door. "Good morning, Mrs. St. Vyr," she said. "I'm Mrs. Syms. I'm your housekeeper. George," she turned to a young man wearing a neatly pressed shirt and pants with an embroidered vest, "Please take the baggage up to the rooms. The saddles can go out to the stables."

The next morning after breakfast, Chloe took a careful walk through the house, her mother's words echoing in her ears. "Strive to become familiar with your environment. Study the area as if it were a battlefield, because it might become one. Learn how to use everything around you for defense, for attack or escape."

Satisfied she knew all the exits and

entrances, Chloe picked up a basket to collect fresh flowers for the house and walked outside. She made a circuit around the edge of the property, noting several trees had branches hanging over the stone fence. She met Henry Miller who was also checking the security of the property.

"That could become a problem security wise," he said, gesturing at one of the trees.

"Yes," she agreed. "One place where we stayed Mom hung bells in the branches of the trees so they would jingle whenever anyone climbed them."

"Not a bad idea," he admitted. "Your mother must have been an unusual woman; not many women concern themselves with those things."

"She and Dad had hunters after them for a year," Chloe said. "I guess you could say she was paranoid."

"What happened to your father?" he asked.

"His enemies found us just before we left for the Portal. He sent Mom ahead with me, intending to follow us after he led them away. He never made it."

"I'm sorry."

She shrugged. "I never had the chance to know him. All I have are my mother's memories of him."

They were passing the front gate when

she heard the whimper.

"What's that?" she asked. She moved toward the sound.

"Be careful girl, if it's an animal in pain it might bite you," Henry protested.

Chloe ignored him. Just outside the gate half hidden under a flowering bush were two small animals. The larger one was about the size of a small Earth cat. The smaller one was obviously young as it was trying to nurse. They had four legs, a long, fluffy tail with a white tip and retractable claws. The creatures had a wedge-shaped head with a pointed nose and big eyes. Their soft, smooth skin was covered in thin red fur.

"It's a fox!" Chloe exclaimed, going down on her knees beside the animal. Although of Vulpine ancestry, she looked enough like the foxes on Earth the colonists had given them the same name. The mother fox looked half-starved and it was obvious she had been beaten badly; one leg was broken and numerous cuts around her head and face were oozing blood. She was nursing a single, still blind kit.

"Oh, you poor thing," Chloe said. "Who did this to you?"

"Chloe be careful!" Henry said again and was again ignored.

Chloe set the basket down beside the animals. Carefully she extended a hand, allowing the mother to sniff it.

"I won't hurt you," she crooned. "I need to take you back to the house so I can set your leg and clean up those cuts. Will you let me do that?"

After a moment, the mother fox licked Chloe's hand. Carefully, Chloe lifted her into the basket, doing the same to the kit as the mother watched anxiously. Once the baby was nestled beside her on the flowers Chloe had gathered earlier, she relaxed.

"She seems quite tame," Chloe said. "Do you suppose she was a pet?"

"Maybe," Henry said doubtfully. "I heard tell of a family who kept them as pets. They said they kept the house free of rodents. Are you planning on keeping them?"

"Why not?" Chloe asked. "You don't think Giselle will object do you?"

Henry snorted. "Considering one of her granddaughters had a pet goat and another a pet goose, I reckon she'll be okay with a fox. Might have trouble with the housekeeper though."

When Chloe brought in the basket with the two foxes, Giselle immediately sent for her medicine box.

"She needs some pain killer first, so she won't get too stressed when we set her leg," Giselle said. "Ask the cook for some shredded meat and eggs. We'll mix the pain

killer with it." Chloe went to the kitchen.

"Henry, I need you to find us some small straight sticks for the splint," Giselle said.

After selecting the proper ingredients, Giselle ground them into powder with her mortar and pestle. They mixed the sedative with the food and offered it to the fox who sniffed it cautiously before scarfing it down.

"It always helps if they are a little hungry," Giselle said. By this time Henry had returned with the sticks, and the fox had dozed off. "I didn't give her much because she's nursing," Giselle said. "So I need you to hold her down while I set the bone."

Chloe put both hands gently on the fox, while Giselle straightened the broken leg. The animal jerked a little, but she didn't come completely awake.

"You see, now the leg must be kept immobile until the bone grows back together," Giselle instructed. She set the two sticks one on each side of the leg and wrapped them firmly with strips of cloth.

"You will need this to make the cast," Mrs. Syms said. "She handed Chloe a bowl of clay thinly mixed with water.

Obeying Giselle's directions, Chloe spread a thin layer of the clay over the bandages.

"It will be dry by the time she awakens," Giselle said, "and it will keep her from attempting to tear off the cast. Now, let's take a look at the kit."

After running gentle hands over the small body and checking the eyes and ears, Giselle said, "He seems to be fine, except I think he's probably hungry. We'll soak some bread in milk to help tide him over."

She handed Chloe a jar of salve. "Use this to clean the cuts on her face and ears," she said.

"I had Mary, the upper housemaid, fix a box with clean sand for her to use as a toilet," Mrs. Syms added. "What are you going to call her?"

"On Earth she would be a Kitsune, a fox, so I will call her Kimi."

"And the baby?"

"Rakki, it means lucky."

Tom, the boy who had been manning the gate came into the room from the kitchen. "A message was left for you, Mrs. St. Vyr," he said, handing her a folded paper.

Giselle opened it. She looked up after reading it. "We are invited to tea with the Woman's Circle," she said. "It will be good for you to meet them Chloe. We must begin to build up the clientele for your medicines and creams. The quickest way is to bring some of them with us as samples.

"Do you have any hand creams?" Mrs. Syms asked? "The girl who does the washing is always complaining about her hands chapping."

"Yes, I do, but I didn't bring a lot with me. I intended to make up more after I arrived. It's easier to buy the ingredients locally than to carry them," Chloe admitted. "I'll just run upstairs and get a jar for her."

When she brought the cream down, Mrs. Syms insisted on paying her a small sum for the cream.

"Oh, but it's for someone in our house," Chloe protested. "I don't think I should charge our workers—"

"Don't be silly girl! you can give us a discount, but you can't give it away for free or you won't make enough money to buy the ingredients," Mrs. Syms pointed out.

Chloe glanced at Giselle who nodded. "Thank you," she said.

Chloe spent the next two days setting up a place to prepare her creams and lotions in part of the area off the kitchen usually used for canning and drying foodstuffs. Since Kimi stuck to her like glue, Chloe started taking Rakki's basket everywhere she went.

Once she had her workspace set up, Chloe turned her attention to creating a space in the garden where she could

practice self-defense. Normally she worked out early in the morning when no one was around, but She hadn't been able to do her daily workout while on board the steamer and her body felt sluggish. As soon as she had selected a good space, she went through the drills. The slow, deceptively graceful exercises and stretches resembled an interpretive dance. As the workout progressed Chloe shifted into the fast punches and kicks making the discipline such an effective hand to hand combat technique.

In preparation for the tea, Giselle advised Chloe to dress stylishly but comfortably in a shirtwaist dress and provided a serviceable white apron to be worn over it.

"Don't put on the apron until after we introduce you," She told the girl.

Giselle had also provided a cleverly made decorated box to transport the creams and lotions. It had slots for each bottle and jar. The slots ensured they didn't rattle around and get broken.

The tea party was held in the ballroom of the Hotel Royal. Chloe was startled to find the number of guests actually filled the room.

"Are all of these women members of the circle?" she asked.

"No, only about twenty of us are

actually active members. Most of them are guests," Amy the local Circle leader said. Amy was about Giselle's age, with a round face, twinkling blue eyes and a plump figure. "We hold these teas once a month to make the women aware of the resources available."

"Chloe! I didn't realize you would be here," exclaimed Lila Dominique.

"Lila, how nice to see you. Are your mother and sisters here as well?"

Lila shook her head. No, just me and Francis. Mother didn't feel well enough to come. Francis, look who's here."

She gestured and a tall, slim girl came to join them.

"Hello Francis," Chloe said. "It's nice to see you again. Are you still staying at the hotel?"

"No, mother finally found a house to suit her," Francis said. "It's on the edge of town, but it's quiet. We have a small garden as well."

"Are you coming to the dance next week?"

"What dance?"

Lila looked surprised. "The Hotel is giving an open dance next Friday night. Mother bought tickets for Francis and me. I think there are still some flyers on the table over there. Mother thinks it's a good way for us to meet people. I hope you

GAIL DALEY

can come so we won't be the only new girls."

"I'll mention it to Giselle," Chloe said. "You'd better take your seats. I think the meeting is about to start."

Amy had walked to the front of the room. She rapped on the podium with a wooden gavel. "If you will all take your seats, I will start the meeting. I want to welcome you all here. If this is your first meeting, please stand and introduce yourself. Chloe, since you are in the back of the room with your samples, why don't you start."

It was a good meeting. Chloe sold almost all the stock she had brought and had orders for that many more. Once the guests had cleared out, the real meeting began.

The remaining members, including Chloe, Giselle and Lizette, gathered at three of the tables in the rear of the room.

"Many of you may not be aware that as well as making cosmetics, lotions and healing potions, Chloe is an experienced investigator," Amy announced. "We're glad to have her here as Councilwoman Grace has something she needs checked out. She will of course pay your usual rates Chloe. Grace?"

A woman of average height, a little on the plump side spoke up. "It's my brother-

in-law," Grace said. "He runs the store my sister and I own. Lately I've begun to suspect he's involved with a criminal gang."

"Yes?" Chloe asked.

"I want to know for sure."

"What kind of activity and why do you want to know?"

"If he's doing what I think he is, both of us could be charged as accessories if he gets caught. I don't think Marissa knows what is going on, but I'd like to know for sure."

"So you want to know two things; if he is committing a crime and is your sister in it with him?"

"Yes, I guess so."

"What crime do you think he's committing?"

Grace sighed. "A friend of my was robbed a month ago. They took a valuable watch; it came from Earth with his parents. I thought I saw it in Sam's shop. Sam shoved it out of sight when he saw me looking at it."

"What makes you think he knew it was stolen when he bought it?"

"They have too much money. I know it sounds petty, but our father used to run the store when we were children, and we barely made ends meet."

"Do you take an active part in running

the store?"

"No," Grace admitted, "but I'm worried I could be considered liable even if I'm just a silent partner."

Chloe studied Grace thoughtfully. She had discussed this aspect of her new career extensively with Giselle. "If I discover a crime being committed, I would have to report it to the authorities," she warned Grace. "Otherwise the local law will arrest me for aiding and abetting a crime."

Grace nodded. "I understand."

"I'll also have to talk to their friends and acquaintances. I always try to keep it quiet, but the fact I'm asking questions about them will probably get out. Are you prepared for the fallout if your sister finds out you're nosing around in her private business?"

Grace was silent, staring at her folded hands on the table in front of her. After a moment she looked up. "Do it. If Marissa gets angry, I'll just deal with it when it happens."

"Okay, I'll take the case."

## MURDER MOST FOUL

THE SHOP DOOR was ajar. It was near closing time and Chloe had timed her visit so she would be able to talk to Adams relatively uninterrupted. A small bell tinkled as she pushed open the door. The interior of the shop was darkened, but she could see bolts of cloth on shelves against the wall as well as tools and other items. All things sold by a general mercantile store. She stopped dead when the odors of blood and death assaulted her nose.

She stepped out of the doorway so her body wouldn't be silhouetted in the light coming in from the street and looked around carefully. The door swung shut silently behind her. Chloe's large dark eyes under the brim of the flowered straw hat she wore, carefully examined every inch of the shop she could see from her place inside the door.

The shop was tidy, and the merchandise neatly stacked on the shelves. A wide wooden counter ran across the back of the room. Behind it was an open door leading into a storeroom.

The smell must be coming from the back of the store. She reached into the new leather handbag Giselle had presented to her. It looked like simply a feminine accessory, however inside it was another matter. Besides pockets for numerous small clay balls holding noxious ingredients to be used against an attacker, there was a holster for a small six gun, and a sheath for a seven-inch knife. She carried a similar weapon in a specially made sheath fitting snugly inside the tops of her Kneehigh boots.

"All my girls carry them," Giselle had explained. "Keep it with you whenever you leave the house."

Chloe reached in and took out the small gun. She had checked to make sure it was loaded before she left the house. Now, she carefully edged her way into the store. There was no dust on the floor to leave tracks, so it was impossible to tell if anyone had recently been in the shop. Everything seemed as it should be.

A stair inside the storeroom led to the second story. Most shopkeepers lived over their stores; after all why pay for two buildings when you didn't have to?

She went around the counter serving as a place for the cash register and a cutting table for the bolts of cloth sold by the merchant.

Here the place wasn't so neat and tidy. A three-tier shelf had been pulled over and pieces of broken jars and ceramic pots littered the floor. A thick glass with a small residue of liquid still in the base had fallen to the floor.

Adams, or what was left of him, lay face up on the floor. A large knife had been driven into his groin several times and the hilt stuck up at an obscene angle.

Chloe scowled at the body. She was no stranger to death. Although she was now attempting to make her living as a herbologist who did part time investigating; Chloe, like her mother before her, had often killed for hire. Still, no death was ever exactly the same.

After checking the storeroom, she went cautiously up the stairs to the second floor. There was no sound but a wheezing snore coming from one of the bedrooms. The upstairs was spotless. It was also apparently empty, except for the bedroom where she heard snoring. A woman, presumedly her client's sister, was sleeping heavily on the bed. A glass with a yellow liquid, smelling faintly of whisky, had a small residue of undissolved powder in the bottom sat on the end table next to the bed.

Leaving the woman sleeping, Chloe went back down the stairs and stood frowning down at Adams body. She was going to have to report finding the dead man, and she wasn't looking forward to it. Her training told her that the person who found a dead body would be considered a suspect by the

authorities.

The bell tinkled and a young boy wandered in.

"Mr. Adams," he called. "Mom sent me to pick up a bag of sugar she forgot—"

He stopped when he saw Chloe.

"Who are you? Where's old Adams?"

"Adams is dead," Chloe informed him. "Please go and get the sheriff or a constable."

"Gosh! Did you kill him?" the lad asked.

"Of course not. I just found him."

The boy came and peeked over the counter. "Gosh!" he said again, his face turning a greenish white. "I thought you were kidding. Is he really dead?"

"Yes," Chloe told him impatiently. "Go on, do as I told you."

When the boy had raced out the door, Chloe stepped to the back of the store. So she had better light to see the body she turned up the gas lamp. She knelt and picked up one of the dead man's hands. The tips of his fingers were red. When she examined his nails, she saw the tell-tale white ridges indicating he had been poisoned. The vomit on the floor under his head smelled faintly of garlic, adding weight to her theory he was dead when he had been stabbed. He wouldn't have voluntarily lain in his own vomit, so she guessed the body had been turned over. To try and help him or stab him? She frowned at the knife. It was an ordinary kitchen knife. In her experience, someone who had been stabbed so many times should have been covered with blood. Adams body showed no bloodstains.

She slipped the gun back into the purse and took out a small weighted string and held it against the knife. The angle was about ninety degrees, with the hilt pointing straight up.

"What are you doing?" a man's voice demanded.

She looked up. Two men stood just inside the doorway. In the shadowy light it wasn't possible to see their features clearly, but one of them stood like a young man. The other seemed older. Both were dressed in the whipcord trousers and homespun shirts worn by most of St. Antoni's male population. Both carried guns in holsters worn on the hip. It was the older man who had spoken.

"Measuring the angle of the blade," she replied.

"What's your name?" the younger of the two asked, coming further into the store. Chloe caught her breath at her first clear sight of him. He was a little over medium height, with a dark, sauterne face. A scar traveled down his cheekbone to his jaw. He exuded an air of tough competency. This man would be a ruthless enemy. He was also the most fascinating man she had ever seen.

"My name is Chloe DeMille," she replied. "Who are you?"

"I'm Sheriff Melody," the older man replied. "This is Enforcer Caleb Jones from Gateway City. We were told there was a dead man here."

"Yes. I believe it's the storekeeper Samuel Adams." She stepped back around the counter, slipping the string with the weight back into her bag. She recognized the name Caleb Jones; the world of her mother's profession on St. Antoni was small. Caleb had been an Enforcer for the Jones family before they had lost Copper City to the Smiths. Before his family lost the war with the Smiths, he had gained a reputation as a ruthless tracker who never gave up a trail. The war with the Smiths had been a bloody war of attrition, with many deaths on both sides. Afterwards, Caleb had gone to work as an Enforcer, but he had continued to hunt for the man who had slain his little sister. A year ago, he had found him hiding in River Crossing. Supposedly Smith had been killed resisting arrest.

Melody glared at her. "Did you touch anything? What are you doing here Miss

DeMille?"

"I came here to ask Mr. Adams some questions," she replied.

Caleb found himself unwillingly fascinated by the woman before him. He had come to Junction City with the firm intention of gently but politely informing this Giselle St. Vyr and her protege women simply weren't suited to the types of work an Enforcer had to do. He was annoyed by the realization of how powerfully he was attracted to her. It had been years since he had been hit with this sharp stirring of desire for a woman. Ruthlessly he subdued it. "About what?"

Chloe hesitated, wondering how much she should share with them. It would be best to stick as closely to the truth as possible, she decided.

"His sister-in-law employed me to find out what he's up to. She has a half interest in the store, and she thought he was trading in stolen goods. She doesn't want to be charged as an accessory if he gets caught."

"He's married?" Caleb asked. "Does he live upstairs?"

"I was told they did," Chloe admitted.

"Where is his wife? Most women would be down here asking us what is going on."

"Your guess is as good as mine," Chloe replied, deciding not to mention she had

found the woman asleep upstairs. In fact it would be better if she said nothing about her exploration of the living quarters.

"Get away from the body. We can't have amateurs messing up the crime scene," Melody growled.

"Unless there is more than one Chloe DeMille in town, she isn't an amateur," Caleb said. "She was recommended to me as a possible Enforcer. Are you the Chloe DeMille whose godmother is Giselle St. Vyr?"

"Yes, that's me," she said. *Giselle had recommended her to work as an Enforcer?* she thought with astonished gratitude.

"I don't like private investigators mucking around in my crime scenes," Melody growled."

Two young deputies entered the store, and he delegated one of them to watch the body while the other went for the local doctor who usually assisted in deaths reported to the sheriff's office. "If that photographer is around, send him along too," The Sheriff added. He started for the stairs. "We need to find the wife. Let's check upstairs. Maybe she's dead as well," he said.

"Have you been upstairs?" he demanded of Chloe who didn't answer him. Melody glared at her one last time before following Caleb up the narrow stairs.

Since she hadn't been given orders to stay behind, Chloe trailed the two men. When she found herself staring at Caleb's powerful legs and shoulders as she followed them, Chloe had to remind herself to pay attention to business. She wanted to know what they thought of what she knew was waiting for them.

One by one, the two men cleared the rooms. Chloe went to the bedroom overlooking the street. The woman sprawled out on the bed hadn't moved. Using her handkerchief, Chloe lifted a used glass on the side table and smelled it.

"What are you doing?" Caleb asked harshly from the doorway.

"This is a Sleeping draught. A pretty strong one," Chloe informed him, setting the glass back down on the table. "From the dried residue in this glass, I'd say she drank it a couple of hours ago."

"So she might have slept through the murder?" Melody asked.

"Probably, or at least been too groggy to check out any noise from downstairs."

"Can you tell what was in the sleeping draught without testing it?" Caleb said, watching her closely.

"From the smell, Bella Dona, Comfrey and a good slug of alcohol," she replied. "It's a commonly prescribed dose for aches, pains or trouble sleeping. To be sure, I'd have to run a few tests."

"What makes you qualified to decide what is in the glass?" Melody asked suspiciously.

She shrugged. "When I'm not investigating, I support myself by selling cosmetics and potions to relieve aches and pains or help someone sleep. Bella Dona is acidy; It should show up in a simple litmus test. Not proof positive of course."

"We'll see if the doctor agrees with you," Melody growled.

Caleb turned up the gas lamp next to the door and the room glared into bright light.

Deciding he might as well go through the motions of evaluating her for the position of Enforcer, he asked, "What is your evaluation of the cause of death in the man downstairs Miss DeMille?"

"I think he was poisoned and already dead when he was stabbed."

"Why do you think that?" Melody asked her.

"There wasn't enough blood," she replied. "In my experience, if the victim is stabbed multiple times there's usually a lot of blood."

"Attended many stabbings, have you?" Caleb asked, eying her speculatively.

She met his eyes squarely. "It's an

occupational hazard in my work."

Melody coughed, interrupting the staring contest. "If Adams was already dead, what killed him?"

"Poison. Something that causes vomiting. He also had red fingertips and white ridges on his nails."

"You touched the body?"

"Only minimally, and only in places that won't interfere in your doctor's diagnosis," she said placatingly.

"Sheriff?" one of the young deputies spoke from the door. "The photographer is here. Can he start?"

"Yes," Melody replied. "And when he's done tell him to come up here too. I want photos of this room. Make sure the glass is dusted with fingerprint powder and photos of it taken. Is Dr. Sanderson here yet?"

"He's downstairs. About done I think."

"Have him come up here and check out Mrs. Adams when he's done down there. I don't want her dying on us."

Melody kept his tone strictly polite when he dismissed her, but it was plain he wanted her gone. "I think we won't need you anymore tonight, Miss DeMille. One of my deputies will see you home. Tomorrow, I'll want you to come into the office and give a statement about what you found here."

"Don't disturb your deputies," Caleb said. "I'll escort her home. I have a few more questions. We can talk on the way."

As they left the store, Chloe glanced over at the young man setting up an old-fashioned box camera behind the counter. Several large bright lamps on pedestals were aimed at the body.

The photographer had a thin, almost feminine face and body. His dark hair was tied back in a man bun. Sharp, ferret looking eyes glanced up as she and Caleb passed him.

Automatically Chloe found herself analyzing his threat potential. Doimer's shirt collar was open and when he looked up to meet her eyes, she could clearly see the young man lacked an Adam's Apple. She kept her revelations to herself and walked toward the door.

Caleb stopped. "What's your name?" He asked the photographer.

"Jeffrey Doimer," the man said. He fished a business card out of his vest pocket and handed it to Caleb.

"Can you make multiple prints of this scene and the one upstairs?"

"I can if you pay for it," Doimer said. "Supplies aren't cheap."

"I'll pay for it. Leave the prints and a bill at the sheriff's office for me."

# SUSPICION

WHEN SHE had found Sam Adams body, Chloe had feverently wished she hadn't agreed to check out his activities. As she waited outside for Caleb to finish with the photographer, Chloe's mind scurried around, testing and discarding various consequences of finding a dead body, and none of them looked good for her. The person who found a body was usually a suspect in the eyes of the authorities. If Sheriff Melody was even close to a competent investigator, he was bound to make queries into her past, and if the Sheriff of Azure City shared his suspicions about her activities for the Women's Circle it could boost her right up to suspect number one.

She was sure inquiries about her would be made, even if it wasn't the sheriff who made them. Chloe had some doubts as to Melody's investigative skills, but she had no doubt whatsoever about Caleb Jones competency. She couldn't have said why she knew this about a man she had barely met, but there was something about his scared face telling her to be wary of him.

When she exited the store, she was startled to see the three massive canines sitting patiently outside. She had wondered why none of the neighbors had

come around to find out what had been happening; she was sure the boy she had sent for the sheriff had told everyone he met about the body. The news would be all over the neighborhood by now. The animals did not seem aggressive, but their size was intimidating. The dogs' presence would have kept the curious away.

"Well now, I wondered why none of the neighbors were curious enough to come over to see what was happening. These guys are impressive; And Scary. Are they yours?" she asked, eying the trio warily.

"Yes, this is Cernunnos, Athena and Aphrodite. They assist me in my work. This is Chloe," he told them. "Friend."

Cautiously Chloe held out a hand for them to sniff. Satisfied she passed inspection; they turned their gazes back to Caleb for further instruction.

Chloe untied her tricorn from the hitching rail in front of the store and swung easily into the saddle. It was time to see how serious Jones was about questioning her.

"I don't need an escort, you know. I'll be perfectly safe mounted on Trisket here. I have a good sense of direction; I won't get lost either."

"I don't agree you would be safe," he said. "Junction City may look safe in the daylight, but it's getting dark. The

criminal classes tend to do their work in the darkness. A woman traveling alone, even on a good tricorn would be thought an easy mark."

"Suit yourself," she said. She turned Trisket and started off at a brisk walk down the street toward home. He mounted with the easy grace of a born rider. His tricorn took a few trotting steps before settling down to ride abreast with her. The three dogs trailed along.

She risked a sidelong glance at her escort. Caleb's facial expression gave nothing away and she wondered what he wanted to ask her. Giselle had recommended her as an Enforcer; perhaps he intended to grill her about her experience as an investigator?

"You said you were investigating Adams activities," he said abruptly. "What did you find out?"

"Why are you so interested?" she parried.

"I'm naturally nosy," he said easily. "I notice you didn't answer my question, Miss DeMille."

"That's right," she said coolly. "You didn't answer mine either."

Caleb laughed, enjoying the game. "The Enforcers are setting up a satellite office here. I'll be heading it up. Naturally, I want to know what kind of

criminal activities I'll need to investigate."

"I thought the Enforcers usually worked with local law enforcement."

"We do. Sheriff Melody is dealing with a series of killings. He requested the Bureau send an investigator to see if there was any connection between the murders. Since I was coming here anyway, my boss suggested I help him out. I'm also supposed to check out the qualifications of any operatives recommended as a candidates for the Enforcers."

"Do you mean you'll be hiring staff?"

"Yes," he admitted. "I'll need a couple of investigators and a receptionist. What did you learn about Adams?"

"I'm sorry, but I can't tell you much about Adams at this point. I just started today, and I have to notify my client to get permission to share anything I found out," she told him.

By this time they had reached the gate of the house Giselle had rented. When she leaned down to tug on the bell, Tomas, Mrs. Pym's son came out clutching a half-eaten sandwich in his hand. Awkwardly, he unbarred the gate to allow Chloe to ride through.

Once inside, she turned to Caleb. "Thank you for escorting me home, Mr. Jones. If you call on us tomorrow

afternoon, I will have had time to speak to my client and gotten permission to tell you what I know."

Caleb watched her ride the tricorn around the side of the house, conscious of a feeling of disappointment. He heard a click as a padlock was snapped closed and glanced down at the boy.

"Are you the gatekeeper?" he asked.

Tomas nodded.

"Do you stay on guard all night?"

Tomas swallowed the bite of sandwich he had been chewing. "No, I was waiting for Miss Chloe to get home."

The boy had been well taught to keep secrets, Caleb thought with some exasperation.

"I'll see you tomorrow," he said, turning to go back to the crime scene.

Chloe rode Trisket around back to the stable, conscious of Caleb's eyes boring into her back as she rode away. She slipped a halter over the tricorn's head and removed the bridle. Trisket was well trained; not as well as her own gruella mare Sinbad but still well taught.

She was unfastening the cinch when one of the newly hired stable hands appeared. "Here, let me do that," he said reaching for the saddle.

Chloe allowed it in favor of brushing sweat off Trisket's back and legs with a soft brush.

"If you want to help, you can put a bait of corn in her manger along with a flake of hay," she told him.

Having settled the tricorn to her satisfaction, Chloe washed her hands and headed toward the house. There was a light on in the parlor. She stopped in the doorway thinking how much the man and woman inside looked like an old married couple. Giselle was working on a piece of delicate embroidery and Henry was reading aloud from a novel.

She was greeted with a series of happy yips as Kimi, her broken leg banging on the floor in her excitement, leaped into her arms, where she proceeded to wash Chloe's face lavishly.

"Yes, I'm glad to see you too," Chloe said laughing, settling herself and the fox into an overstuffed chair and propping her feet on a footstool.

"You're later than we expected. How did it go tonight?" Giselle asked. She poured Chloe a cup of lukewarm tea and handed it to her.

Chloe accepted the cup gratefully and took a sip. "Not so good. Adams is dead."

Henry stopped reading to look at her gravely.

"Oh?" Giselle eyed her.

"I didn't do it."

"I didn't suppose you did. How did he die?"

"Poison," she said briefly. "My guess is he was already dead when someone stabbed a knife in his groin about eight or nine times. He'd been dead about four hours when I got there."

"Does the Sheriff agree with you?"

Chloe leaned her head back against the chair. "The doctor agreed as well."

Giselle frowned. "What makes you think he was already dead when he was stabbed? I always thought multiple stab wounds mean a crime of passion."

Chloe took another sip of tea, absently stroking Kimi's sleek back. "Usually you would be right. The reason I think he was already dead when he was stabbed is because there wasn't enough blood on the scene. If he had been alive when he was stabbed, there would have been blood everywhere."

"I see. Someone will need to send a message to Grace. Was her sister there when it happened?"

"Yes, but she had taken a strong sleeping draught and I doubt if a war going on downstairs would have woken her."

"She isn't still in the house?"

"No, the doctor said something about taking her back to his office."

"Good, we can wait until morning to

tell Grace about it."

"An Enforcer came to the store with the Sheriff. His name is Caleb Jones. Have you heard of him?"

"Yes. I used to live in Copper City before the war between the Smith's and Jones broke out. The Jones Clan lost. I had heard Caleb had gone to work as an Enforcer. Be careful around him; he's good at what he does."

"He says he's here to set up a satellite office for the Enforcers," Chloe said. "He was mighty curious about what I was investigating for Grace. I need her permission to let them know what I've found out so far, otherwise they'll think I'm obstructing the investigation."

Giselle eyed her shrewdly. "You like him," she said.

Heat rose in in her face. "He's—different," she said.

"You don't fool me, girl. I have three granddaughters. I can read it in your face and voice. You're attracted to him."

"Yes," Chloe admitted.

She was more than attracted; she was fascinated, she admitted to herself as she brushed her hair the requisite one hundred strokes before retiring to bed. She heard her mother's voice echoing in her ears, "Don't let yourself be blindsided by how attractive you find a man" Angela had

warned her. "Make damn sure he isn't your enemy before you give in to it."

"Dad was your enemy," Chloe had protested. "You fell in love with him anyway."

"Yes, I did," Angela admitted. "By the time I realized I was in love, I was sure I could trust him. He was able to accept what I do; very few men or women can do that."

## SHADOW OF A KILLER

A FEW MINUTES after Caleb and Chloe left, Sheriff Melody came downstairs. He stayed out of the photographer's way studying the crime scene intently. His presence didn't bother Jeffry Doimer, who liked photographing crime scenes. The blood and gore accumulating at murder scenes didn't bother him; in fact over the past few months he had grown to like the metallic smell of freshly spilled blood.

"How soon will those be ready?" Sheriff Melody asked.

"If I work on them tonight, I can have them ready in the morning," Doimer responded. "You wanted me to do the upstairs too?"

"Just the bedroom and the kitchen. Mrs. Adams is alive, but I want a photo of the glass with the sleeping potion after it's been dusted, and I want a general layout of this room and the one upstairs in case we need to review them later."

"I'm going to need a couple of deputies to help me bring her down," Doctor Sanderson called from upstairs.

"Are you taking her to your clinic?" Melody asked.

"Yes, I want to keep an eye on her while she sleeps it off."

A few minutes later the two young

deputies came downstairs, each carrying one end of a makeshift stretcher. They took Mrs. Adams out to a waiting rickshaw. The doctor's voice could be heard giving instructions to take the woman to his clinic.

"Tell the nurse I said to put her to bed and keep an eye on her," he told them.

Melody left Raymond Cortez, one of his deputies. to oversee Doimer and walked outside where he put a "police business, do not enter" seal on the door.

Caleb arrived just as Melody finished. It wasn't yet finalized; Cortez would activate the seal when he and Doimer left.

"What did you do with Mrs. Adams?" Caleb asked.

Melody shrugged. "The Doctor took her back to his offices in a Rickshaw. She's in no shape to answer questions anyway. Did you find out anything from Miss DeMille?"

"Not much more than she said here, she intends to contact her client to ask her permission to share any information she's picked up."

Melody snorted. "She found the body. Think she had anything to do with his death?"

Caleb checked an impulse to leap hotly to Chloe's defense. "I don't think so," he said, keeping his voice non-committal.

"She was recommended to my boss in Gateway City as a recruit for the Enforcers."

"So she's one of us," Melody said. "Doesn't put her above suspicion but it knocks her down some. I'm heading in for the night. You got a place to stay?"

"Not yet. I'm hoping you could recommend one. I also need a place with an office and a stable attached for the new office."

"There's an empty store front across from the Sheriff's station. Living quarters upstairs and a couple of stalls in the rear. The guy who owned it died last month. I think his widow is looking to sell or rent it out."

"It sounds good. Is she still living there?"

"No, Mrs. Tobiason went home to her mother. Mike Lewis is handling the property for her. He usually eats dinner in the Broken Spoke. We can probably still catch him."

Lewis was not only willing to rent the space, but he suggested Caleb sleep there tonight.

"You can put the tricorns up in the Sheriff's Office stable for now," Melody offered. "And there's a good take out place next to my office. You can pick up dinner for yourself and the dogs there."

Happy with his arrangements for the

night Caleb woke up in a good mood. The Cafe Melody had recommended was already open, so he crossed the street and ordered breakfast. He also ordered a takeaway order for the dogs. "You can drop the empty pail back here later this morning," the owner said.

Chloe's morning hadn't started so well. Grace had come around after breakfast, and as Chloe had expected, her client wasn't pleased with the news her brother-in-law had got himself killed the night before.

They were sitting in the parlor drinking the tea Giselle had poured. Kimi was sitting on Chloe's lap while the kit slept in a basket at her feet.

"Who killed him?" Grace demanded.

"I don't know. I don't think the Sheriff does yet either."

"Is my sister likely to be a suspect?"

Chloe sighed. "Maybe. You see, Adams died of some type of alkaloid poisoning. The stabbing happened after he was dead. If the poison was recently ingested, she's probably not a suspect since she was out cold from her sleeping draught. If the poisoning occurred over several weeks or days, yes, it's possible Marissa could be implicated. It's a truism in investigative circles to always look at the spouse first in a suspicious death."

"Dammit," Grace said.

"Did Marissa have any reason to want her husband dead?"

"I don't know," Grace admitted. "Their marriage was—odd."

"Odd? In what way?"

Grace hesitated before answering. Finally she said, "I have some reason to think their sex life was violent."

"Violent? How?"

"She told me he liked to choke her during sex."

Chloe's eyebrows rose. "And she liked it?"

"Apparently."

"Well that isn't a reason to want him dead," Chloe pointed out. "Did he play around on her?"

"I heard a few rumors, but I don't know for sure. Marissa got angry when I asked her about it."

"I'll need a list of the names of the women," Chloe said.

"Why do you want them?"

"It's a place to start. If he cheated on his wife, he probably cheated on the others too. Or somebody's husband or brother might have objected to his attentions. You never know."

"Alright. How much of this is going to be made public?"

"Well, I won't be talking to any newspapers, but I do need to share what I

find out with whoever is investigating the murder. Otherwise I'm interfering in the official investigation."

"Alright," Grace said reluctantly. "I suppose you have to."

After Grace left, Chloe and Giselle looked at each other. "She had a motive as well," Giselle said.

"Yes, I know. It isn't as strong as her sisters, but losing a big source of income is a motive."

"What are you going to tell Enforcer Jones?"

"About Grace? She wants me to find out who killed him."

She stuck to this; when Caleb arrived promptly at noon Kimi took immediate exception to the enormous dogs, getting between them and Rakki's basket and barking a shrill challenge.

"Whoa," Caleb said, to the fox. "It's okay. They won't hurt your baby." He turned and pointed to the wall beside the entryway. "*Eisteddwich, arhoslad*," he told the trio, who obediently sat down and waited.

"You give them commands in Welsh?" Giselle asked.

"Yes, it prevents enemies from attempting to confuse them. I'm surprised you recognized the language," he said.

"I spent a lot of time in Wales growing

up," she replied.

"When did you arrive in St. Antoni?" he asked.

"We arrived at least thirty years ago."

"We?"

A shadow darkened her face. "Myself, my husband and my son. My husband was murdered the first week. They never found out who did it."

Chloe picked up Rakki's basket and put the kit in her lap. Kimi jumped up to join them, still glaring at Caleb's entourage.

"What happened to her leg?" he asked, pointing at the cast Kimi still wore.

"I'm not sure. It was broken when I found her and Rakki," Chloe said.

"Would you like some tea or coffee?" Giselle asked.

"Coffee would be great," Caleb replied. "It's been a long morning."

He turned to Chloe. "Did you speak to your client?"

"Yes, she gave permission to tell you what I find out, but she would prefer it not be made public knowledge if it can be helped."

"Understandable," he said. "A lot of dirt gets brought out during a murder investigation and most of it is irrelevant."

Mrs. Syms appeared in the doorway, hesitating when she saw they had a visitor.

"I believe lunch is ready. Would you like to join us, Mr. Jones?" Giselle asked.

Caleb smiled at her. "Yes, I would. I haven't had a home cooked meal in several months.

Any discussion of the murder was tabled until after the meal. During which Chloe was amused to see that in a gentle ladylike way Giselle was interrogating Caleb about his lifestyle and habits.

Apparently, he passed inspection because she invited him to accompany herself, Chloe and Henry to the dance on Friday.

"The dance will be a good way for you to meet a lot of people," she said.

"Thank you. I'd be delighted to be one of your party," he said. "Is it formal?"

"It's supposed to be an open invitation, so I imagine there will be many different styles of dress worn," Chloe said.

When they were back in the parlor, Caleb asked Chloe what her plans were for the day.

"Grace gave me a list of women she suspects Adams was involved with. I thought I would start there."

"He was a lady's man?"

"Well, she had heard rumors, but she

didn't have any proof and her sister told her it was none of her business when she asked about them."

"Mind if I come along?"

"Not at all. I warned her I would have to share whatever I learned with the investigating officer."

She gave orders to have Trisket saddled and brought around front. After handing Kim's basket and Rakki over to Giselle she went upstairs to put on her hat.

When she came down, she and Caleb went outside, accompanied by the echo of Kimi's displeased barks when the three large dogs rose to follow them.

"Where do you want to go first?" Caleb asked.

"One of the women operates a photographic studio near Adams' store. I thought we would go there first."

What do you know about her?"

"According to Grace she is new to Junction City. She is a widow. Her name is Lynda Darnell and she has three teenage boys."

The studio was across from Adams' mercantile. The large window in the front displayed several types of photos, ranging from colorful landscapes to a few portraits.

"This is a good section of town," Caleb observed, eying the neatly kept wooden

boardwalks running along in front of the stores. Besides Adams Mercantile and the photography shop, there was a florist with a colorful display of vases and potted plants, several cafes serving pastry's and coffee, a dress shop, a tailor and a harness and saddle store.

When they entered the photography shop, a tall graceful woman looked up from a ledger. She was about forty, with light hair drawn back in a neat bun. "Do you have an appointment?" she asked.

"No we don't. We're from the Sheriff's office," Caleb replied.

"We would like to speak to you about the murder that happened in the mercantile store yesterday," Chloe added. "This is Enforcer Caleb Jones, and my name is Chloe DeMille."

Darnell looked wary. "I didn't see or hear anything yesterday," she said.

"Alright," Chloe said. "Your name was mentioned as being one of Samuel Adams friends. How well did you know him?"

"I wouldn't exactly have called him a friend," Darnell said. "In fact I only met him when I opened the shop a couple of weeks ago. He wanted me to take a portrait of himself."

"Did he try to date you?" Chloe asked.

Darnell made an exasperated sound. "Yes, he invited me out to dinner."

"Did you go?" Caleb inquired.

"I did. I wasn't aware at the time that he was married. I broke it off when I discovered it."

"How did he take that?"

"He didn't like it." A boy in his early teens had come from the back of the store. He had the gangly build of a youth just entering puberty with a tanned complexion and a shock of near-white hair. He was dressed in jeans and a short-sleeved red shirt.

"What is your name?" Caleb asked him.

Darnell put a protective arm around the boy. "This is my middle son John."

John shrugged his mother's arm off. "It's okay Mom," he said.

Caleb looked at the boy. "You look like a smart lad. Did you hear anything about the murder yesterday."

"Sure," John said. "It was all over the street. Tim Grimes told everyone about it when she," he nodded at Chloe, "sent him for the sheriff."

"What about before he told you anything?"

"No, I was in back putting up some supplies that had come in."

"Were you present when your mother told Mr. Adams she had no intention of seeing him again because he was married?"

"My brothers and I were upstairs," he

replied. "We came down when we heard the noise."

"What kind of noise?" Chloe asked him.

He glanced at his mother and received a nod from her. "He was attacking Mom when we got there. Larry and I tried to pull him off her, but we weren't strong enough. Tony ran upstairs and got Dad's old pistol. He put it against the back of Adams' neck and told him to get off her."

"What did Adams do?"

"He got up, but he told Tony he didn't think he would have the guts to shoot him. Tony handed Mom the gun, and she told him *she* wasn't afraid to use it. Said he was to go and not come back."

"Did Adams leave?"

"Yes, but he was pretty mad. He said he would ruin Mom's business."

"Did he try Mrs. Darnell?" Chloe asked.

"I don't know," the woman replied. "It's always slow starting in a new location, but my business is looking up. We booked three appointments for family portraits this morning."

"Did he try to choke you?" Chloe asked. Caleb gave her a startled look.

"When he had her down on the floor, his hands were around her neck," John said. "Is that what you mean?"

Chloe nodded. "Thank you for speaking to us. Did you have anything else Caleb?"

"No, that is all for now, but we might need to talk to you again," he said.

After they left, Linda looked over at her son. "You told them more than we agreed on."

"I think Enforcer Jones would have found it out anyway," John replied. "He's a dangerous man. I wouldn't want to cross him."

"So is she," his mother replied. "She camouflages it better though."

Out in the street, Chloe and Caleb mounted their tricorns. "Where to next?" Caleb asked, signaling the dogs to follow them.

"I would like to talk to Susan Fisher next," Chloe said. "She and her husband have a house a couple of blocks from here."

"If she's married, Adams liked to live dangerously. I wonder if her husband knew about the affair?"

"I suppose we'll have to speak to him as well," Chloe said in resignation. She looked over at him. "Not to change the subject, but what did you think of Lynda Darnell?"

"I think she was telling a part of the truth," he said.

"What part of what she told us do you think was a lie?"

"I don't think any of what she told us was a lie, but I do think there is more to

the story."

"Do you think he raped her, and the boys only came upon them afterwards?"

"Maybe. It would give her a motive to poison him. Especially if he was trying to ruin her business."

"What about the stabbing?"

"I think that could have been done by another person entirely—" He broke off abruptly. "We're being followed."

Chloe glanced casually around the busy street. "Who is it?"

"It's Sheriff Melody's photographer," Caleb said.

"I wonder what he wants."

Caleb gave her a nasty grin. "Let's find out. When we reach the next corner, turn in and wait. When he follows us, we should be able to catch him and ask him some questions."

Once they were in the alley, Caleb dismounted and handed Chloe the reins of his tricorn. He stepped over against the wall and waited.

Doimer came rushing around the corner and stopped dead. He turned as if to run, but Caleb caught him by the back of his coat and hauled him back.

"I think we need a little privacy for our discussion," he told Doimer.

"Let me go! I haven't done anything!" Doimer said shrilly.

"You've been following us all morning. I want to know why," Caleb said.

"I know you're investigating Adams' murder," Doimer said with a sullen glare. "I was hoping to get some photos of whoever you interview. My paper will pay me well for information about the investigation. But my editor likes photos to go with it."

"If photos of anyone we interview shows up in any newspaper, I'll arrest you for interfering in the investigation, and Melody won't employ you to take any more crime photos," Caleb warned him. "Do you understand me?"

"Yeah, I understand," Doimer said.

"And for heaven's sake stop following us around like a sick puppy," Chloe told him. "I don't like it."

Doimer looked up at her. Nothing much showed in his face, but she could feel the puff of sheer rage aimed at her.

Caleb apparently sensed it too, because he shook Doimer like a rat. "You heard her. Stop following her around. It will be the worse for you if you don't, understand?"

When Doimer simply glared at him, Caleb gave him another shake. "I didn't hear you."

"Yeah, I understand," Doimer's voice was venomous.

Caleb let him go and Doimer scuttled

back around the building.

When they rode out of the alley, Chloe stopped abruptly. Caleb turned back impatiently. "What is it?"

Chloe urged Trisket into motion to join him. "I'm not sure, but I think Doimer might not have been the only one following us. This is the third time I've seen Larry Dominique today."

"Who is he?"

"His family came in on the same steamer we did. Giselle, Lizette and I shared a room with his wife and daughters. I thought Lila told me he had a job as a bookkeeper."

Caleb frowned. "Unless his new employer sent him out on three different errands the same day, which I think is unlikely, I agree there's reason to be suspicious. Who did his daughter say he was working for?"

"Some steamship company down on the docks, I think."

"So there isn't a reason for him to be this far uptown. I'll be going down there later to talk to some of the workers, I'll ask around. And no, it's better if you don't accompany me."

"If you're going to ask them about Adams—"

"This doesn't concern the Adams murder. I told Melody I'd assist him with some

prostitute murders he's dealing with. I think the dock workers will talk more freely if I don't have a woman with me."

"The case you came to Junction City to look into," she said. "I forgot Adams' murder isn't your only case. If you're sure you don't want my help, I think I'll go back to the house and write up my notes after we speak with Susan Fisher."

"About this other case; I realize an investigator isn't in the same line of work as the women who were killed, but your appearance matches their general description. Would you object to taking one of my dogs with you when you are away from the house?"

"A lot of women have dark hair and eyes," she said.

"I know," he said. "But like me you've just moved here though so you may accidentally find yourself in the area they worked in."

"I'll think about it," she said.

## A GLITTERING EYE

SUSAN FISHER, their second person of interest, lived in a large mansion in an affluent suburb. Like the house Giselle had rented, this home had a wall to provide privacy and a gate. The gatekeeper used by the Fishers wasn't a ten-year-old boy, but a grizzled veteran who wasn't disposed to allow them to enter.

He glared at Caleb's badge as if it offended him. "What do you want here?" he asked truculently.

"If your mistress wants you to know, she'll tell you," Caleb retorted. "Now open the gate and announce us or I will arrest you for interfering in an open investigation."

He got a glare in return, but the man said, "Wait here. I'll see if she wants to talk to you."

About five minutes later, he returned and grudgingly opened the gate. "You can tie your tricorns out front," he said. He eyed the three large dogs suspiciously. "Those can stay outside with the tricorns. Mrs. Fisher doesn't like large dogs."

Susan Fisher received them in a formal parlor. She was dressed in a shirtwaist blouse and bell-shaped skirt. A large ruby ring decorated her right hand, and her left was adorned with a wide gold band and a large diamond engagement ring. Her blond hair was neatly wound in a coronet and her large blue eyes regarded them warily.

"Daniel said this was about an open investigation. I can't imagine what you think I know about any investigations."

"This is about the murder of Samuel Adams," Caleb said.

His shock tactics worked. Mrs. Fisher turned pale and sat down hard on one of her overstuffed chairs, clutching her throat with one hand.

"Oh, my God," she said.

"I understand you had a close relationship with him," Chloe said.

Mrs. Fisher swallowed before she spoke. "It wasn't exactly a relationship," she said. "Oh my God, what if Gerald hears about this?"

"Would he be angry?" Chloe asked.

"Not on my account," Susan said, "but he will be angry if there is a scandal."

"How did you meet Samuel Adams?" Chloe asked.

"I was shopping with a friend and she wanted some material he had in his store," Susan told her. "We flirted a little and one thing led to another. It didn't mean anything. I was bored, and a little angry with Gerald because he wasn't paying attention to me."

"What makes you so sure your husband

wouldn't care if you slept with another man?" Caleb asked.

Susan gave him a glance of acute dislike. "It had happened before. He didn't care the first time so why would anything change? You see, my husband didn't marry me for love; he married me for my father's connections in the shipping industry."

"He might not love you, but he might care about the blow to his pride," Caleb pointed out.

"Not enough to commit murder about it," she replied.

Chloe studied her thoughtfully. "Did Adams ever choke you during sex?"

A flush rose up her throat to her forehead. "Yes," she said. "It made it more exciting. He never hurt me, and he stopped if I asked him to."

"Did you ask him to?"

"Not often," she said. Her flush had died down. "If there is nothing else, I'd like you to leave."

Plainly the interview was over.

"You realize we will have to speak to your husband?" Caleb said.

"Oh my God, must you?"

"I'm afraid so," Chloe said. "You might want to get whatever story you intend to tell ready for him."

"We might need to speak to you again,

as well," Caleb said. It would make it easier if you told your gatekeeper to let us in if we come back."

"Why should I make it easier for you?" she flashed. "Oh, alright, I'll tell him to let you in if you come back here. Just, Go, please."

They didn't discuss the interview until they had left the Fisher's grand house.

"Giselle said there is a coffee shop near here. I don't know about you, but I'm thirsty and I'd like a little time to let that interview settle before we move on to Mary Jessup."

"Alright, I could use a cup of coffee," Caleb said.

He was pleased to note a water trough near the cafe. It was a warm day; the dogs and the tricorns swallowed large amounts of water.

"You know we will have to do a follow up with Gerald Fisher don't you?"

"Yes," she admitted, sipping her coffee. The beverage wouldn't have passed for coffee on Earth , but the highly spiced beverage contained a similar amount of caffeine. "I would like to hold off on questioning him until tomorrow though give her a chance to tell him about it herself. I don't want to ruin the marriage if we can help it."

Caleb leaned back, stretching his legs

out into the aisle. "I suppose if he already knows about it waiting a day won't matter, and if he doesn't, he wouldn't have a motive to kill Adams."

"How did you become an Enforcer?" Chloe asked changing the subject.

When he hesitated, she said quickly. "It's alright if you don't want to tell me. I was just curious."

"I was always an Enforcer of sorts," he said. "When the Jones family ran Copper City, I worked for them. After we lost the war with the Smiths, I went to work for the Consolidated City State Law Enforcement Bureau."

"I'm sorry," she said. "How many of your family made it out of Copper City alive?"

He drank more coffee. "Myself, several cousins and a couple of aunts."

"What about your parents?"

"They died some time ago. I had a younger sister, But she was murdered by Jacob Smith just before the war started." He made a wry grimace. "In a way, you could say her murder started the war."

"She was murdered by one of the Smiths, wasn't she?"

"Yes," he replied. "We demanded they turn the guilty party over to us and they claimed they didn't know who it was. We had statements from the cafe owners where

her body was found. The man's brother and his wife gave him an alibi for the time it happened. It was a lie and we knew it. There was a fight in a bar over it and people from both families were killed, and out of the blue we had a full-scale war on our hands."

Chole studied him. She instinctively knew Caleb Jones wouldn't have let his sister's murderer go unpunished.

"Did you catch the man who killed your sister?" she asked.

"Yes," he said. "Last year I received two messages telling me he was hiding out in River Crossing under a different name. When I arrived to take him in, he pulled a gun on me."

He said nothing else, and Chloe didn't ask any more. Caleb was here and alive, so his sister's murderer must be dead.

"How did you come to be an investigator?" he asked her.

Like Caleb earlier, Chloe hesitated over how much to tell a comparative stranger. She decided to tell him a portion of the story. He had told her a part of his; fair was fair after all.

"Back on Earth , my mother was a corporate spy and sometimes an assassin. She was good at her job, but she made a fatal mistake. She fell in love with a man she was assigned to kill, and her bosses turned on her. She and my father hid out underground on Earth until I was born. The hunters never gave up on finding them though, so my parents decided to escape from Earth through one of the Portals. I'm not sure why they chose St. Antoni to run to, unless it was the fact no records are kept on Earth of who moves there. The night they were going to leave, the hunters found them. My father sent my mother ahead with me, planning on joining her after he'd led the hunters away. He never made it. The skills making Mom so good at her job on Earth made her an equally good investigator here. She started teaching them to me as soon I was able to learn them."

"What happened to her?" he asked.

"She was killed on her last assignment. I was with her, watching from concealment. I saw him kill her. I threw my knife at him and got him in the throat. He died. I was only thirteen."

"It must have been hard, being left on your own when you were barely a teenager."

"It was," she admitted. "But thanks to Mom, I have some marketable skills. Not pleasant ones, but I am able to support myself."

"Yet you are changing cities and starting over," he remarked.

Chloe's chin lifted. "I'm not ashamed

of how Mom and I earned our living. It put food on the table and kept clothes on our backs. I just decided I wanted to help people. When Giselle offered to sponsor me here in Junction City, I jumped at the chance. She is introducing me as an apothecary and an investigator to the Women's Circle here. Finding out what Sam Adams was up to for his sister-in-law was my first case."

"Did you know Giselle St. Vyr also recommended you as a candidate for the Enforcers?" he asked.

"Oh," Chloe said softly; a warm tingling feeling flowed into her. He had mentioned the recommendation the first day, but she hadn't been sure he intended to follow through with an offer. "You mean I would do what you do?"

"Well, I think the idea was for me to hire you as a deputy when I set up this branch office."

Chloe quickly pulled herself together. "Is that a job offer?" she asked.

He nodded. "Working as an Enforcer requires skills most women don't learn. I'm satisfied you do have them. We'll see how this case tracks; we may find we can't stand working together."

She grinned at him. "I'll try harder if you will."

"You need to stop by the Sheriff's

office and sign your statement," he reminded her as they left the cafe.

"We might as well get it done before we go on to Mary Jessup," Chloe said.

Mary and Jase Jessup lived with his parents. They timed their arrival at the Jessup residence for late afternoon when the men would be at work.

They were shown into the parlor. Mrs. Jessup senior was a tall, stern-faced woman with a liberal amount of grey showing in her hair. The younger woman was slight, blond, and exuded an aura of deference to the older woman.

"Why do you want to talk to Mary?" the older woman demanded.

"We are investigating Samuel Adams murder," Chloe explained. "We are trying to talk to anyone who was in the vicinity of his shop the day he was murdered day."

"What does his murder have to do with Mary?"

"According to the other shopkeepers, Mary usually walks there when she took the baby out for an afternoon stroll. We want to know what she saw on her walk."

"She didn't see anything," Mrs. Jessup said.

"If you don't mind, we would like to hear Mary's answer," Caleb intervened. By mutual agreement, they had decided to allow Chloe to handle most of the

interview, but he realized, if he didn't step in the older woman would control anything the younger one told them.

"She would have told me if she'd seen anything out of the ordinary," Mrs. Jessup stated.

"It might not have been out of the ordinary," Chloe said soothingly. She turned to Mary, "What I would like you to do is let your mind go back to that afternoon. Tell me what you see."

After a slightly scared look at her mother-in-law, Mary Jessup said. "It was time for his nap, and Davy was fussing a little so I thought some fresh air might relax him. He likes the sights and sounds of the stores."

"A lot of babies do," Chloe encouraged. "What is the first thing you remember about the street?"

"The first place we stopped was the Flower Shoppe. Mrs. Sanderson was watering the plants in those big tubs under the window. I like to smell them. I hope someday to grow my own flowers, so I asked her about watering times, and the best times for planting."

"I've told you we can plant a window box here," her mother-in-law said.

"I know, Mother Jean," Mary said with a placating smile. "But Jess is hoping we can move into our own place soon. We just

need to save a little more."

"Did you notice anyone going into Adams Mercantile?" Caleb asked.

Mary frowned a little. "The woman who runs the new photography shop went inside. She came out just as Davy and I started down the boardwalk. I noticed her because after we get our own place, I want to get a family portrait done of the three of us. Most of the people I saw weren't exactly strangers; I usually see them on our walk, but I don't have names for them."

"Alright," Chloe rose from her chair. "If you remember anything else, please contact me." She handed Mary one of her new business cards.

Once they were back out on the street, Caleb said, "You didn't ask her if she knew Adams."

"Not with that female dragon sitting there. Even if the rumor about Adams and her is false, she would be too frightened of her mother-in-law to say anything. I'll have to try and catch her when she takes her afternoon walk."

Caleb nodded. "Just remember to take Athena with you."

Chloe nodded resignedly. She had given in on the idea of taking the enormous dog with her on her investigations. Caleb had spent some time teaching her the commands Athena would respond to and she was

confident she could control her.

"What are you going to do?"

"I'm going to go down to the docks to have a talk with her husband. I want to know what he knows about Adams. I think he would be more likely to talk to me if I'm alone anyway."

"Would he say anything? After all, he married her despite any gossip."

"We'll see."

When she got home, she rushed into the parlor and gave Giselle a hug accompanied by Kimi's welcoming yips. "Thank you," she said. "Caleb just told me you recommended me for a job as an Enforcer."

Disentangling herself from the strangling hug Giselle laughed. "You're welcome. Did he offer you a job as deputy?"

"Sort of. He said we needed to work together on this case so we can decide if a job would work out long term."

Giselle frowned. "Well I suppose it's a step in the right direction."

Over dinner, Giselle reminded Chloe she needed more Decumaria oil to make more lotions and creams. "Caleb's job offer was a little vague to suit me. You can't afford to neglect your bread and butter income while he's deciding about hiring you."

"Yes, I know," Chloe replied. "I'll send a runner to let Caleb know he's going to have to question Gerald Fisher by

himself tomorrow."

"There is a large hedge of Decumaria outside of town where you can harvest the petals and the stems to turn into oils," Giselle said. "I'll give you directions."

## TREADS THE SHADOW

THE DECUMARIA hedge was everything Giselle had said it would be. An enormous splash of color in reds, yellow, blues and purples stretched out for several miles. It did look a little like the rose hedge in one of the children's fairy tale books her mother had brought with her from Earth. Some story about a princess sleeping behind a hedge of roses. The Decumara flowers were layers of petals resembling a vase. She knew the petals could be pressed to extract the oil. She would use the oils in some of the cosmetics and medicines Giselle was teaching her to make.

She dismounted and picketed Trisket so she could graze on the lush grass on this side of the hedge. Athena laid down and went to sleep in the shade of the trees nearby.

"Don't go around to the back side of the barricade," Giselle had warned. "Behind the hedge is a swamp. Only a real swamp rat can guide you through it. There are quicksand pits, poisonous plants and some nasty swamp snakes living in the swampy water."

As she laid out her supplies for harvesting the plants, Chloe was conscious of a faint prickling on the back of her

neck told her she was being watched. Again. She made a frown of distaste. The watcher was undoubtedly Jeffrey Doimer again. Doimer didn't frighten Chloe. She didn't know what his motive for keeping such close tabs on her was, but she was sure Caleb was wrong when he said Doimer was interested in her. Doimer didn't watch her the way a man watched a woman he wanted sexually. The way Caleb watched her.

Putting on leather gloves to protect her arms and hands from the thorns and waxy ooze protecting the Decumaria, she cut the plants she intended to use, separating them by color so none of the oils oozing from the stems could mix together. The stems of the plant were most useful in creating medicines, but if the oils in them mixed uncontrollably, the resulting muddle could produce unpredictable results.

When she harvested the right amount of each color, she wrapped the ends in the waxed cloth she had prepared for this purpose, and wrapped up the whole bundle in a loosely woven burlap sack.

When she had gathered the amount of plants she wanted, she threw the bundles over the back of her saddle, tying them down with the leather strings dangling from the saddle skirt.

When she finished tying the bundle on

the offside, she went around Trisket's rump and saw Athena stand up and look beyond her, her ears pricked forward. Doimer had come out of hiding. He was standing about twelve feet away.

A sudden rush of anger hit her. She hadn't liked the uneasy feeling he had given her watching her from hiding. She dropped Trisket's reins, knowing the mare had been ground trained and stomped towards Doimer, outrage in every line of her walk.

"What do you think you're doing?" she demanded. "I'm getting pretty sick of you following me around. Stop it." Athena, who had followed her, growled. Getting no reprimand, she growled louder.

Doimer cast a wary eye at the dog, but gave her an oily smile. "Why does a man usually follow a pretty woman around?"

Chloe snorted. "But we both know I'm not your type, don't we?"

Doimer stared at her in shock. "What do you mean?" he whispered.

Chloe shrugged. "I've worn enough disguises to recognize one when I see it. You should always wear a bandana over your throat, so your lack of an Adams apple doesn't show. I saw you didn't have one that day in the store when you were photographing Samuel Adams body."

His teeth drew back in a snarl, and he

reached for her. "I won't let you tell anyone else."

Chloe grabbed the long slender fingers and twisted hard. She continued to twist until Doimer went down, flipping over on his hands and knees to relieve the pressure on his arm and fingers. Seeing him with his butt sticking up in the air, Chloe gave in to her temper and put her boot on his rump and pushed. Doimer ended up face first in the prickly weed patch in front of the hedge.

Athena growled again, and looked up at Chloe, obviously waiting for permission to act.

"Try to grab me again and I'll break your hand," she told him. "Athena, *Dewch.*"

She turned her back on him stepped up into Trisket's saddle. Riding away she was reluctantly followed by Athena. When she looked back, Doimer had turned over and was sitting on the ground. When he looked up to glare at her, she thought she saw the sheen of unshed tears in his eyes. He wiped dirt and weeds off his face. Frustrated anger roiled off him, and she knew nothing would have pleased him more than to see her dead.

"I'll kill you if you talk about me," he hissed.

"I won't tell anyone your secret unless I have to," she said. "But just so you

know, if you keep tailing me, I might decide telling someone what you are is necessary. Quit following me around. I don't like it."

She left him sitting there and rode back toward town. She met Caleb coming to meet her.

While Chloe had been harvesting Decumaria plants, Caleb had joined Sheriff Melody in questioning some friends of the dead prostitutes. None of them had been forthcoming about the victim's activities. While this was understandable, it had also been frustrating.

After he left Melody, Caleb had gone by Giselle's house to see Chloe and drop off some dog food for Athena.

"She went out there alone?" he demanded.

Sensing his upset, Giselle said soothingly. "She took your dog with her. She should be fine."

"How long ago did she leave?" he asked.

"She went out about nine this morning. She should be on her way back by now."

"Give me directions to get there," he said.

Giselle rolled her eyes at masculine silliness, but obliged.

When he turned and left without saying farewell, Giselle frowned after him. Caleb Jones wasn't a man to give in to unnecessary worry; either he had already fallen for Chloe, or was there a real reason to be afraid for her. She decided she needed to ask Henry if there was any especial danger to Chloe.

Caleb set off for the hedge at a brisk lope. Being able to act soothed him somewhat. There was no reason for the killer to target Chloe, he reminded himself; she wasn't a prostitute. But they *had* been followed the day before. When he met her, placidly trotting along the road and obviously safe, he was angry all over again.

"Giselle said you came out here to harvest plants. What were you thinking, coming out here alone? It isn't safe until we know why Doimer has been watching you."

Chloe eyed him warily. She could tell he was furious with her. "I don't know why he's been watching me, but I'm in no danger from Doimer," she said placatingly. "I can handle her."

Caleb was momentarily distracted from the roiling fear consuming him on learning she had gone out alone. "Her?" he asked. "Do you think Doimer is a woman?"

"I'm not sure he/she knows," she said coolly. "I'm sure there is a woman's body under those clothes. However, whoever is wearing them thinks and acts like a man. I think he hates women because he's trapped in a woman's body, and he hates men because they have what he doesn't."

"So much anger could make him dangerous," he pointed out. "If he decides to blame you—"

She nodded. "I know. I promise I'll be careful. What did you do today?"

Caleb took a calming breath and allowed himself to be diverted. He had sense enough to recognize yelling at Chloe wouldn't get him anywhere. "After the sheriff and I re-questioned some of the local girls who work the same areas as the murdered prostitutes, I talked to some of the dock workers about Fisher."

"Did you learn anything?"

"According to them, he's got a quick temper and he likes to fight. A couple of weeks ago he got into it with a worker who answered him back and he almost beat him to death. Word is he had to pay the man while he was off recuperating so he wouldn't press charges."

"Guilty conscience?"

"The men think it was so the man he beat wouldn't press charges."

"Doesn't sound like someone who would use poison to take out a rival," she said.

"I agree. If Fisher knew about the affair, he would have been more likely to confront Adams and beat Hell out of him."

"Well, at least we can cross him off,"

she said. "It still leaves Mrs. Fisher with a motive. She might have been afraid of what her husband would do to her if he found out."

Caleb shook his head. "She told him Adams attacked her, remember? From what he said, he believed her story."

"If he believed her why *didn't* he confront Adams?"

"That is a good question. It would have been more in character. I think we need to look more into Adams business connections. Fisher might have thought Adams was protected by someone he didn't want to cross. I need to talk to Sheriff Melody and find out who runs crime in Junction City and pay him a visit."

"How do we get in to see him?"

"Get this straight: there is no *we* in this part of the investigation. You are not going with me when I talk to a crime boss."

"We're partners in this investigation," she reminded him. "You can't leave me out of any part of it."

He glared at her in frustration. He had spent enough time with Chloe to realize she would simply find a way to question the crime lord on her own if he didn't take her with him. "Oh, Hell. I'll come by after I talk to the sheriff this afternoon and we'll make plans."

"Excellent. I'll tell Mrs. Syms you'll be joining us for dinner, shall I?"

When Caleb dropped her off at home, Chloe took her harvest inside, setting it down on the counter in the canning area. Like most houses on St. Antoni, off the kitchen was a large area used for the preparation of drying, smoking, canning and otherwise preparing foods for the winter months. The large room had storage shelves filled with clay jars and pots, and wax to be melted to seal the contents. A large drying rack with a shelf under it held bluestones to be heated to aid in the drying sat off to one side. In the other corner where it would easily vent to the outside, was a smoker for drying and smoking meat and fish.

After changing into an apron to cover her work clothes, she spent a productive afternoon, stripping the petals off the Decumaria flowers.

These she spread out on the drying screen and set them inside the dryer. She wouldn't need heat to dry them, just air.

The stems she cut up and set aside for the oils to drain out into a clay pot so they could be collected and stored.

She had found the rhythmic sameness of preparing the creams and lotions worked well as a form of meditation. She had often used it when she was working out how to

accomplish a job.

Chloe admitted to herself Caleb's offer of a position as an Enforcer was something she wanted.

He was also here to evaluate her as an investigator, but he had been devoting almost all his time to helping her solve Adams murder. If she was going to become and Enforcer, she needed to prove she was a capable investigator on her own. If she helped him with the prostitute murders, it would go a long way to proving she was a good investigator on her own. She decided to ask Caleb about the deaths of the prostitutes. If she questioned them without male law enforcement hanging over them, the women might be persuaded to tell her things they hadn't wanted to tell the law.

# SMOKE & MIRRORS

CHLOE HAD every intention of trying to catch Mary Jessup on her walk the next day, but as Giselle pointed out, Life had a way of interfering with plans. Two days before the dance, Giselle looked in Chloe's closet and decided the girl had nothing suitable for a formal dance.

"This dance is going to be your first social appearance in society here in Junction City," Giselle said. "It's important to make the right impression on your prospective customers."

After going through the clothes Chloe had brought with her, Giselle decided a visit to her favorite dressmaker was in order.

They went to Belinda DuSalle's Dress Emporium. Like many of Giselle's acquaintances, Belinda was a member of the Woman's Circle. The dress emporium was located on a street just off the main thoroughfare. The viewing room in the back boasted a rarity on St. Antoni—a three-sided mirror enabling the viewer to see all sides of the dress without contortions.

"Giselle! How lovely to see you again so soon," Belinda exclaimed when they walked in the shop. "Is this another of your granddaughters?"

"Chloe is the daughter of an old

friend," Giselle said. "She is moving here to set up shop selling cosmetics and lotions. We will be attending the dance at the Hotel Royale on Friday. I'm hoping you have something suitable for her."

"And for you as well?" Belinda asked archly.

Giselle smiled. "Perhaps. What do you have already made?"

Belinda walked around Chloe her mouth pursed thoughtfully. "You have a lovely figure," she said. "Susan," she spoke to her assistant, "bring out the rose gown, the one with the lace fringe around the bodice."

The dress was calf length and fit snuggly at the waist, belling out in a graceful arc, emphasizing Chloe's hourglass figure. Cream lace edged the low-cut bodice enough to show off her full breasts and the elbow-length sleeves draped gracefully on her toned arms.

"Giselle needs a new dress as well," Chloe told Belinda. "Something to impress Henry."

"Who is Henry?" Belinda asked.

"Henry Miller," Chloe said with a smile. "He escorted us to Junction City. His partner married Giselle's granddaughter Bethany last summer."

Belinda gave Giselle a knowing eye. "Is he handsome?"

"Not exactly," Giselle said, looking a little uncomfortable. "I like his looks, but I would say he looks like the kind of man you can depend on."

"His kind of man is hard to find," Belinda said. "Let's pick you out a beautiful dress."

For Giselle, she pulled out a softly draped violet ensemble, with chiffon draped to cover her breasts and loose sleeves of the same material for ease of movement. Giselle still had a good figure and the dress, with its full draped skirt and snug bodice showed it off to perfection.

When they got home from the dressmaker, Mrs. Syms had tea waiting for them. Mary took the new clothes upstairs to hang in the closets.

While Chloe was cutting up plants and trying on dresses, Caleb was having an uncomfortable chat with Sheriff Melody who wasn't happy with what Caleb had to say. "Are you sure about this?" he asked.

"The list of women came from Adam's sister-in-law. Chloe and I spoke to Mrs. Fisher yesterday and she admitted it."

"Fisher's on the city council," Melody said glumly.

"Do you want to cry off going with me to question him?" Caleb asked.

He got a glare in return. "Nobody's

above the law, Jones. Let's go do it. This time of day Fisher should be over in his office at city hall."

The City hall was an elaborate three-story structure. The top tier held offices of the minor clerks and rooms to store files. Below were the offices of government officials. The bottom floor was made up of court rooms and meeting areas.

Fisher's secretary, a slim young man in a 'dress for success suit' didn't want to let them in to see his boss.

"Why don't you tell him we're here and let him decide?" suggested Melody.

After some hesitation, the young man finally did as he asked. His surprise when Fisher himself came out to greet them was apparent. Fisher was dressed in a neatly pressed suit with a conservative tie. The suit was of good quality but not expensive. He didn't want to look too prosperous to his constituents. He was a medium built man, with soft white hands and a neatly trimmed beard and mustache.

"I always have time for our local law enforcement," Fisher said heartily.

"Thank you for making time for us," Melody assured him, following him into the office and closing the door. "Although, strictly speaking, Caleb here isn't local. He is an Enforcer from the City State Marshall's office."

The lines around Fisher's eyes tightened a little. "I'm pleased to meet you Marshal—?"

"Enforcer Caleb Jones," Caleb corrected him. He sat down without being asked in one of the client chairs.

"You've got a nice view, Fisher," Caleb added.

"I like it," Fisher said. He studied them a moment, before he said, "I don't think I'm getting a visit from two high-ranking law enforcements officials just to visit. What can I do for you gentlemen?"

"What can you tell us about Samuel Adams?"

"Which one? I know of at least three men with that name."

Fisher was a cool character, Caleb thought. "The Samuel Adams that ran Adams Mercantile on Fifth street."

"Oh, him." Fisher scowled. "The man's a lowlife who goes around attacking women."

"You know this from personal experience?"

Fisher tapped his fist on his desk. "Yeah, I do as a matter of fact. About a month ago he ran into my wife when she was out riding alone out by the Decumaria Hedge. She had stopped to pick a few flowers. He rode up and started a conversation, then attacked her. She got away from him before he did much more than tear her blouse."

Caleb's eyebrows rose. "A month and you haven't done anything about it? I would have thought a caring husband would have at least filed charges."

"Susan only told me about the incident last night after you came to visit her. It's a good thing he's dead. If I had found out when it had happened, I'd probably be in jail for assault."

"Why do you think your wife waited so long to tell you about the attack?"

"Our private life isn't any of your business," Fisher snapped. Without warning his arrogance deflated. "My wife and I— well we've sort of drifted apart lately."

"Just so we have things official," Melody interjected, "Where were you last Monday night?"

"Playing poker with a group of friends down at Joe's Bar."

Caleb and Melody exchanged glances, and Caleb stood up. Melody followed suit. "Thank you for your time Councilman Fisher," Caleb said. "I'll let you know if we need more information from you."

Fisher continued to smile genially until the door had closed behind the two lawmen. He had known from the beginning Melody was an honest man if not a clever one. Melody's lack of cleverness was why

he had backed him for the office of Sheriff. This Enforcer from Gateway city was a different kettle of fish. Fisher judged Jones to be both tough and smart. He was going to be much harder to fool than Melody.

Problems were beginning to crop up in his plan to take over Junction City. Susan was a silly woman, but he didn't suspect her of anything but being a fool. Damn Adams anyway. The man had dared to lay hands on his property, so he had to be killed to ensure no one else made the same mistake, but the timing was lousy. The body shouldn't have been discovered until Adams' wife woke up from her sleeping draught. She would have had no alibi, and the death taken as a domestic quarrel; the result of Adams lifestyle. But the woman investigator had thrown a wrench into the plan when she arrived right after his man had made sure Adams was dead and driven the knife into the dead body several times. The DeMille woman had told the Sheriff Adams had been poisoned. Rumor would have attributed the death to his lifestyle and the Sheriff would have accepted the domestic violence theory.

That damn Hercule Jones, a small-time crime boss, had been nosing around too, trying to discover who the Big Man (Fisher's alter ego) was. Jones, he

thought, was it a coincidence the new Enforcer and Hercule had the same last name? He pictured the two faces in his mind and swore. If the two men weren't related, he would eat his hat. This put a new complexion on the affair. Perhaps Hercule Jones wasn't just trying to muscle in on his business. Maybe the man was an undercover Enforcer. It was time to take steps about him.

On the way back to the Sherriff's Office, Melody glanced over at Caleb. The Enforcer's face was hard to read. "You believe him?" he finally asked.

"It's possible," Caleb replied. "I'll need to check with the bartender at Joe's Bar to see if he remembers Fisher being there."

"I know," Melody sighed. "From all accounts, Gerald Fisher is a hot-tempered man who doesn't hesitate to throw a punch. I can't see him using a weapon like poison, though. If he knew about his wife being attacked, I think he was much more likely to try and beat Adams to a pulp."

When they reached the Sherriff's office, Caleb noticed Mike Lewis, the agent who had agreed to rent him his new headquarters, waiting across the street.

"I need to go and see what he wants," he told Melody.

The sheriff nodded. "I've got some

thinking to do anyway. Keep me in the loop."

Caleb nodded and led his tricorn across the street.

"Hello, Mike," he said. "Do you have keys for me?"

"Yes, I do. I sent your deposit to Mrs. Tobiason. When she accepted, she asked me to let you know she is open to selling the property outright."

"If I like the place, I probably will do that, but I want to stay there a couple of weeks before I make a decision. I need to contact Enforcer Headquarters anyway. It will probably take a few weeks for them to get back to me."

The bottom half of the building was divided into sections. The front would do as a reception area, as soon as he cleared out some of the shelving, Caleb decided. The rooms to the left would do as offices for himself, Chloe, and the third, as yet unknown, investigator. The rearmost rooms would work as a breakroom for the staff and a storage area for the files he knew would accumulate.

"This looks good," he told Mike. "I'd like to see the stable area next; I have tricorns and dogs I'll need kennel space for."

The stable had five stalls, a room for tack and a loft so feed could be loaded on

a platform and raised to the loft by use of a pully. A bachelor apartment with two bedrooms was overhead.

"Does that work?" Caleb gestured to the pully platform.

"Yes, everything works," Lewis assured him.

"I understand you will be needing furniture and staff to run the office?"

"Yes, I'll need a receptionist, a cook and someone to take charge of the stables and kennel. Can you recommend anyone?"

"You can hire staff from Jacob Binns down on main street. He runs a sort of informal employment service."

"Good. Let's see the upstairs."

The living quarters were simple; a kitchen with a dumbwaiter descending to the lower floor, two bedrooms and a living room. He was delighted to learn Mrs. Tobiason had left behind most of the upstairs furnishings.

"Did she take what she wanted when she left?" he asked Lewis.

The man shrugged. "Her mother has a fully furnished house, so she didn't need most of it. She said you could use the stuff while you rented, and if you bought the place, she would sell it to you."

After settling his staff issues with Binns and being assured he would have a cook ready to start in the morning, and a

receptionist and stableman available by the end of the week, Caleb's next stop was a feed and grain store where he arranged for a delivery of feed for the animals.

The proprietor of the carpentry shop Lewis had recommended, Les Swann, had a desk and several chairs that could work in the reception area ready to go, and promised he could have two more desks ready in about four weeks. Until they were ready, Caleb would have to make do with kitchen chairs for any visitors.

His living quarters arranged; Caleb decided he would have time to see Jessup before his shift ended. Jase Jessup was a medium sized young man, about twenty, with brown hair and a sun darkened complexion. The sleeves of his homespun shirt were rolled up to show muscular forearms. He eyed Caleb with some unease.

"Forman says you want to talk to me, Enforcer? What about?"

"I'm assisting the sheriff with Samuel Adams murder," Caleb told him.

At the name, Jessup's face tightened. "I barely knew the man. Why ask me?"

"Your wife knew him," Caleb replied. "He was paying her considerable attention before and after she married you."

Jessup's face turned purple, and he took a hasty step forward, clenching his fists. "What do you mean?"

Caleb didn't move. "It means he was chasing her. If she complained to you, you might have been annoyed enough to do something about it."

Jessup settled back on his heels. "Mary's an innocent in some ways. I could tell he was after her even if she didn't realize it."

"Did it cause a fight between you?"

"She got mad when I told her he wanted to bed her," Jessup admitted. "Said he was a married man and he just liked to flirt." He snorted. "That ended for her when we got married."

"From what I've heard your marriage wouldn't have stopped him from paying her attention. What did you do about it?"

Jessup scowled. "I didn't have to do anything. Mary doesn't go out alone anymore. Besides, we have a baby."

Caleb waited patiently. He knew from experience silence could be a goad.

Finally Jessup spoke. "Look," he said. "I knew he was starting to hang around her again and she was afraid of him. I was making plans to take care of it."

"What kind of plans?"

"I was going to wait until he headed down to the bar where he hangs out. I am a lot younger than Adams, and I've had my share of brawls, I figured a good beating would send him a message to stay away from

her."

"Did ask anyone to side you while you—er—sent your message?"

"Of course not. I don't want to spread gossip about my own wife," Jessup exclaimed.

"Where were you last Monday?"

"Monday night is my baseball practice night. Mary brings the baby out to watch us. She can tell you I was there. Afterwards I dropped in at Smokey's Bar and Grill to hang out with my team. I got home around midnight."

Caleb wasn't fully satisfied with the man's answers but until he heard back from Chloe about what Mary Jessup said when she didn't have a nosy mother-in-law looking over her shoulder, he had to let it go.

"I may have more questions," he told Jessup. "Don't leave town without notifying me. You can reach me at the Marshall's office across from the Sheriff's office."

## DANCE UPON THE AIR

WHEN FRIDAY arrived, Chloe and Giselle spent most of the day in preparation. Giselle had given the staff the night off in case any of them wanted to attend the dance.

Mrs. Syms smiled, "Not for me. I think I'll take the evening off and relax with a good book. The Runners brought in a bunch of new novels from Earth this time."

Henry was already downstairs in the parlor when Caleb arrived. He had dressed in a dark tailored coat and striped waistcoat, topped off with a freshly pressed grey shirt and pants.

Caleb had dressed in a similar outfit, but his shirt was a dark red, the vest was light brown and so were the pants and coat.

Knowing the men would be waiting in the hall, Giselle let Chloe descend the stairs first. She enjoyed the stunned expression on Caleb's face when he first saw Chloe. Her matchmaking was coming along fine there.

"Wow," was all Caleb said. "You look— beautiful."

"Why thank you," Chloe said, flushing a little under the male admiration in his eyes.

"This will be my first official dance— back in Azure City Aunt Marie thought I was too young. I went with the family, but mostly it was to keep an eye on the children." She was aware she was babbling, but for some reason the warm look in Caleb's eyes made her feel awkward and ill at ease.

"I'm out of practice as well," he admitted. "It's been years since I attended a purely social affair. I hope I don't trip over my own feet on the dance floor."

His answer relaxed Chloe and made her feel less self-conscious. By the time they arrived at the Hotel, she was feeling much more like herself.

The Hotel Royale prided itself on being the premier event location for Junction City. Tickets for the monthly open dance were five copper chips each and there was a strict dress code; no working attire was allowed. The ballroom was large enough to hold over five hundred attendees. The floors were highly polished wood enabling dancers to glide across its surface with ease. Lighting from five enormous chandeliers descended from its ornate ceiling. Long banquet tables loaded with delicious finger foods ran along the wall leading to the kitchen. Around the edge of the room, interspaced with some chairs for the nondancers, the staff had set up a series of small and large tables where guests could sit out a few dances.

Each guest's name was announced when they arrived. Amy Wong hurried over to them when Giselle's party arrived.

"I'm so glad you could make it," she exclaimed. Amy was a tiny, five foot nothing with a nicely rounded figure. Like Giselle, she had aged well.

"Come and be introduced to the people at our table."

As they moved through the crowd, Chloe spotted Lila and Francis sitting with a group of people and waved a greeting.

When the musicians started up a waltz, Caleb held out his hand. "Dance, Chole?" he asked.

"Yes, thank you," she said. Marie Nguyn had made sure all her children knew how to dance. Since Chloe had lived with them after her mother was killed, she had considered Chloe 'hers', so she had been included in the lessons.

"Dancing is a social skill you all need to know," Marie had said firmly, when some of the boys objected.

Dancing with Caleb was different from dancing with one of her adopted brothers. She was sharply aware of the feel of Caleb's large hand on her waist as he spun her around in the intricate steps. Even though the layers of his coat, vest and shirt, she felt the hard muscles of his shoulder under her hand. She resisted the

urge to move her hand along his arm, but she wanted to feel more of him.

"I can tell you are an accomplished dancer, Chloe," he said. "You don't need to concentrate on the steps to keep time."

Startled, she looked up from the button on his shirt where she had firmly fixed her eyes, to find he was smiling down at her.

"It isn't that," she said. "The only other men I've danced with were Marie's sons and nephews. It feels different with you."

"Good different, or bad different?"

"Different," she replied. "I haven't decided which yet."

He gave a warm masculine chuckle of satisfaction. "Good, I'll do my best to convince you dancing with me is good different."

Insensibly, Chloe relaxed into the familiar steps of the dance. When the music stopped, Caleb walked her back to Amy's table.

"Shall I get us some punch?" he asked.

"Yes, please. Nothing alcoholic though."

"He's a handsome man," Amy said, observing that Chloe watched him as he walked away.

She flushed. "Yes," she admitted, "he is."

As the leader of the local Women's Circle, Amy Wong had a wide acquaintance so there was a constant flow of visitors at her table.

Chloe was sipping a cup of fruit punch and nibbling on a few of the h'orderves Caleb had brought over from the buffet table when Lila and Francis joined her.

"Isn't this exciting?" Lila asked. "I've met so many new friends."

"Not all of them will turn out to be friends," Francis said. Despite being two years younger, she was the more pragmatic of the sisters. "Mother is more interested in finding husbands for us than in us making friends."

"You're both too young to be thinking of getting married immediately," Giselle remarked. "I wouldn't be in too much of a hurry if I were you."

"Mother is anxious to get us off her hands," Francis said. "She thinks men want younger women. I think she is afraid we'll turn into old hags if we wait."

Giselle laughed. "All three of my granddaughters were in their twenties when they married. Bethany was nearly twenty-eight. I assure you, both of you will only grow lovelier when you've grown up a little. You will also know better what you want in a husband with a little experience under your belts."

"You came with the new Enforcer," Lila said to Chloe. "Are you going to marry him?"

Chloe choked on her punch and Giselle had to slap her on her back. "I do like him a lot, but he's going to be my boss in the Enforcers, so a romantic relationship could be tricky."

"I envy you having a career," Francis said. "Mother won't hear of any of us training for any kind of job."

"Do you want to work?" Chloe asked.

"I want to be independent," Francis said. "I want to earn my own money, so I don't have to marry someone I don't like."

"If you don't have any training, about the only jobs open are things requiring a lot of physical labor," Chloe warned her.

"I know," Francis said. "I was hoping you could help me get some type of training that mother won't think of as a job."

"Like what?" Chloe asked.

"I saw a demonstration of a typewriter at school once. It looked fascinating. I think if I could learn it, I might be able to get a position in a law firm as a clerk."

When Caleb returned with more punch for himself and Chloe, he was accompanied by a tall blue-eyed man Chloe recognized as one of the deputies who had been on duty when she found Adams body.

"Chloe you remember Deputy Raymond Cortez, don't you?"

"Yes, of course I do. Deputy, have you met Miss Lila and Miss Francis Dominique?"

Deputy Cortez smiled at the girls. "How do you do? It's a pleasure to meet such lovely newcomers to our city. I think there is a new number just starting Miss Lila. Would you care to dance?"

"Yes, Thank you," she said.

"I think your sister has made a conquest," Giselle said.

"Probably," Francis said, adding, "It won't do him any good unless he makes enough money to satisfy Mother though."

"Money isn't the most important thing in choosing a husband," Chloe protested.

Francis smiled a little wryly. "It is to Mother. I think she is obsessed with us making good matches."

The man who had been conversing with Mrs. Dominique came over to where they were seated. His arrival coincided with Lila and Cortez's return to the table. He was about medium height, with neatly cut brown hair with just a touch of grey. He wasn't bad looking, but something about him set off Chloe's radar.

"Ah, here you are Lila," he said holding out his hand. "I believe this is my dance."

Lila forced a smile and took the hand

being held out to her. "Of course Mr. Judson."

Francis gave a realistic shudder. "Mother thinks he's a good prospect," she said.

"You don't like him," Chloe observed.

"No, I don't. I just wish—"

"Wish what?" Chloe asked.

"Lila doesn't like him either, but I think she's going to marry him if mother orders her to."

"What about your father?" Giselle asked. "What does he think of Judson?"

Francis shrugged. "I don't think he cares much about us. He usually lets Mother run anything having to do with us.

"What kind of relationship do you girls have with him?" Giselle asked.

"I hate to admit it, but I don't know him well. He was gone most of the time we were small children. We even made the trip to River Crossing to catch the steamboat without him."

"I didn't know that," Chloe said. "I thought you had been living around River Crossing."

Francis shook her head. "No, we were living in Azure City when mother got the letter telling us to book passage on the stage travelling along the coast road to take us to River Crossing. He met us there. This is the first time he's lived with us in a long time. He's gone all day, so we don't see much of him."

The current dance was another waltz and Chloe noticed Francis was keeping a close eye on her sister and Mr. Judson's progress.

"Francis," Chloe asked, "What's the matter?"

"I overheard Mother tell Lila to go with him if Mr. Judson asked her to go someplace private with him. On the way over here, Lila asked me to follow and interrupt them if they left the floor."

"Why doesn't she just tell him no?"

"She's afraid of Mother," Francis replied. "I think Mother hopes to catch them in a compromising position so she can force him to marry Lila."

"That only works if he is an honorable man," Chloe reminded her.

"Oh, no! there they go," Francis exclaimed. She rose hurriedly and tried to go across the floor to reach her sister, but the rapidly moving dancers prevented her from taking a direct route across the room.

"Find Caleb and send him after us," Chloe whispered to Giselle, as she rose and followed the younger girl. The movements of the dancers forced Chloe to also use the edge of the dance floor to keep from being run over.

Judson had taken Lila into an unoccupied meeting room. Francis had pushed the door open. Over her shoulder, Chloe could see Judson had Lila backed up against a wall, pulling at her clothes.

"No, Please don't," Lila gasped. "No, I don't want to—"

He slapped her across the face. "I paid your mother for you! If you fight me, it'll be the worse for you."

Francis rushed into the room. "You leave her alone!" she cried, attempting to pull him away from her sister.

He shoved Francis away, and she stumbled, tripping and falling on her backside.

Chloe calmly took the delicate looking lady's pistol out of the purse dangling on her wrist. Detouring around Francis's prone body, Chloe put the pistol against the back of Judson's neck and cocked it.

"Back away from Miss Dominique," she ordered softly, "or I'll blow your head off."

As Judson did as he was told, Chloe backed away from him, circling just out of his reach to put herself between him and Lila.

He glared at her. "This is none of your business, girlie," he spat. "I paid her mother to be able to pop her cherry."

"I seriously doubt she would agree for

you to use her daughter without a wedding taking place," Chloe told him. "Her mother wants her to make a good marriage. She's not selling her daughter to you to use as a whore. Now get out and don't come near these girls again."

"You won't shoot," he said. "You haven't got the guts."

Chloe grinned at him. "Want to bet your life on it? I've got six bullets in this pretty toy and I'm a damn good shot. I think one in your balls, one in your heart, and one between the eyes should do it."

"That's a little bit of an overkill," Caleb said from the doorway. "Why waste two extra bullets?"

"Because I want him to know even if he lives over it, he'll never rape another woman," She retorted.

Caleb reached down and helped Francis up off the floor. "Suit yourself," he said. He looked at Judson, "If I were you, I'd get out while the getting's good," he advised.

Cursing under his breath, Judson stomped out the door.

Chloe uncocked the pistol and rolled the cylinder back to an empty chamber before tucking it back into her purse.

"Thank you, Caleb," Chloe said. "I might have needed to shoot him if you hadn't come in when you did."

She turned to the sisters. Lila had her face hidden in her hands, sobbing softly. One of the tiny ruffled sleeves on her dress had been ripped, and a bruise was already forming on her upper arm.

"Take her down to the lady's retiring room, Francis," she said. "It's just down the hall. Ask the maid for a needle and thread to repair her sleeve. I'll be along and help restore her hairstyle in a moment."

When the girls had gone, she turned to Caleb. "I don't think Francis heard him, but he said he paid their mother to use Lila. Her father should hear about this so he can return any money or jewelry Judson gave Cora Dominique."

He nodded. "I agree. Suppose you let me handle telling her father?"

"Please," she said. "I'm sure the information will come better from a man than if I told him."

When she reached the retiring room, Chloe found the attendant reattaching Lila's sleeve, while Francis combed out her sisters deshelvished hair and pinned it back into its original style. Lila was holding a wet rag to her cheek where Judson had slapped her.

Francis looked up in alarm when the door opened, but relaxed when she realized it was Chloe and not her mother.

"Chloe where can I get a gun like yours?" she asked.

"Do you know how to use a gun?" Chloe asked.

"Not yet, but I can learn if you'll teach me," Francis said grimly. "I don't like being helpless."

"Alright," Chloe agreed. Because of her mother's tutoring, by the time she had been ten years old, handling deadly weapons had been second nature to her. She couldn't imagine not being able to defend herself against an attack. "Can you come by early tomorrow morning? I'll give you some basic lessons and we'll arrange to get you a weapon. Wear riding dress, to practice firing, we need to go out into the countryside. Henry showed me a place to practice shooting down by the river."

Caleb had watched Judson's retreat with a frown. Chloe had humiliated the man and Judson was the kind who would want revenge.

Telling Chloe to watch out for Judson wasn't likely to make much difference in her behavior; Caleb had already figured out Chloe was too fearless for her own good. He couldn't stop her taking chances, but he could provide additional protection from Judson or anyone else Chloe offended during this investigation. He caught her hand as she and Francis were leaving the retiring room.

"Just a moment. I want you to promise to always take Athena with you if you are away from the house."

Chloe frowned. "I already take her almost everywhere with me, but there are times when it isn't convenient, like tonight."

"A little inconvenience is worth your safety; Judson is the kind who holds grudges. He's not above lying in wait for you. Athena will provide extra protection if he tries anything."

Chloe sighed. The request made sense, even if she wasn't thrilled with the prospect of being followed around by the enormous dog.

She returned to the dance with Francis and Lila. Deputy Ortiz immediately claimed Lila for another dance. Knowing she would be safe with the deputy, Chloe relaxed.

"What happened?" Giselle asked. "You were gone nearly twenty minutes, and you've covered it with makeup, but I can see where someone smacked Lila."

"That awful man, Judson did it," Francis said.

"Why?" Giselle said.

Francis flushed in embarrassment. "I think he might have misunderstood what mother said to him. I think *she* thought he was asking if Lila was a virgin because he

wants a virtuous wife."

"From what he said when he tried to rape Lila, he thinks Mrs. Dominque sold her to him; not as a wife but as a drab," Chloe said.

"Did Judson actually pay her money tonight?"

"I think he must have," Francis said. "Mother has this special pocket in all her dresses where she keeps a money bag. I'm sure I saw her put something in it when Judson left her to ask Lila to dance."

"Caleb intends to tell the girl's father about the attack," Chloe said. "He was sure Mr. Dominque will make his wife give back the money."

Giselle sighed. "They'll muff it," she said. She looked around and spotted Cora Dominique over by the punch bowl.

"Stay here and keep an eye on those two," she said, indicating Francis and Lila.

"What are you going to do?"

"It's time Cora and I had a little chat."

"What did she mean?" Francis asked.

"Giselle doesn't have much faith in men's powers of persuasion when it comes to making a women do something she doesn't want to," Chloe said. She patted Francis's hand reassuringly. "Your name won't come up, I promise."

When he left Chloe in the retiring room, Caleb went looking for Lila's father. He found Larry Dominque in the card room.

"Larry Dominique?" When the man looked up from his cards, Caleb continued. "I'm sorry to interrupt your game, but I need to speak privately with you. It's about your daughters."

Dominique frowned up at him. "What about them? My wife usually deals with anything to do with them. You should speak to her."

Caleb laid his hand on the man's shoulder. "I must insist if you please."

For just an instant something dark and deadly flashed in Dominique's eyes. It was gone so quickly, Caleb wondered if he had imagined it. He took a step back when Dominique, laid down his cards and stood up.

"If you will excuse me, Gentlemen," Dominque said.

"I think there is an empty room off this one," Dominique said.

"After you," Caleb replied.

Inside the room, Dominique turned around. "Now what did you want to say to me?"

"What do you know about Levi Judson?"

"He's a businessman around town. I met him at one of those society teas my wife dragged me to. Why?"

"He's not a nice man, and he is also married. He seems to be under the impression your wife sold him your oldest daughter so he could use her as a whore."

Dominque frowned. "Cora wouldn't do that. My wife intends for our daughters to make good marriages."

"That isn't what Judson said when I interrupted him trying to rape Lila," Caleb said.

"Well, what do you expect me to do about it?"

Caleb stared in astonishment. In this man's place he would be ready to kill anyone who molested his daughter, if he had one. Dominique appeared almost indifferent.

"You need to make your wife give back the money. Or better yet, get it from her and give it back to him yourself."

A few minutes earlier, Giselle had said much the same thing to Cora Dominique. Finding the other woman sipping punch, Giselle gripped Cora by the arm. "We need to talk privately," she said.

Cora was flushed with triumph. "What about?"

"About you selling your daughter to be a whore," Giselle said, not mincing words.

"I did no such thing! Just this evening, I negotiated an advantageous

marriage for Lila."

"Not with Levi Judson," Giselle said. "He has a wife in Copper City. Besides, he thinks he's paid money to use her, not to marry her."

Cora stared at her. "That's not true! I don't believe you! You're just jealous because your little protégé can't land a husband."

"Don't be an ass," Giselle said. "Francis and Chloe both overheard Judson tell Lila he bought her. It isn't marriage he has in mind; just sex. Once Judson uses her like a whore, he'll pass her on to one of his friends; you won't make a good marriage for her when it comes out he used her sexually."

Cora had opened her mouth to argue when Caleb and Larry Dominique walked up. Caleb stood back with his arms folded, watching Dominique and his wife.

"Did you take money from Judson for Lila?" Dominique asked her.

"He made a dowry payment for her," Cora said.

"From what I hear, that isn't what he thinks he's bought." Dominique held out his hand. "Give me what he paid you, and I'll return it."

Cora stared at her husband, wondering if she dared defy him. Larry had a dark streak of viciousness. He seldom showed that side of himself to her, but she had been married long enough to sense when it was coming to the surface.

"Oh do as you please, ruin your daughter's chances!" she snapped. She reached into a hidden pocket in her gown and pulled out a small drawstring bag. She emptied most of it out into her husband's hand. "There, are you satisfied?" she demanded.

"We will talk about this later," Dominque said.

"I saw Judson in the bar," Caleb said. "Do you want me to come with you?"

"I suppose so," Dominique said.

Judson eyed Dominique and Caleb warily when they found him. Reluctantly, he took the small pile of coins and gemstones when Dominique handed it to him.

"My wife misunderstood your intentions, Judson," Larry said. "I'm sorry for the misunderstanding; my wife and I intend for our daughters to make good marriages. Since I understand you are already married, a marriage to my daughter won't be possible."

"Stupid milksop!" Judson sneered when Dominque walked away.

"Don't be too sure about that," Caleb said. He added, "I don't expect to hear any barroom gossip about those girls, Judson."

Judson glared at him. "When did the Enforcer's office care about a woman pimping out her daughters?"

"When her daughter and her sisters are friends of the woman I'm going to marry."

## SUNSHINE & SHADOW

DESPITE THE late night, Chloe was up at dawn as usual to start her exercise routine. This morning, the gate bell rang just as she was about to leave by the kitchen door. She looked out the window and saw it was Francis.

Amused because she thought the girl had shown up so early because she was excited to begin her lessons, Chloe and Athena walked down to the gate to let her in.

"You're here early," Chloe remarked.

"I thought it would cause less of a fuss if I was gone when Mother and Lila wake up," Francis explained. "I left Mother a note saying you had offered to teach me how to make the hand cream she liked so much."

"I thought she didn't want you learning a trade," Chloe said.

"She doesn't, but she likes saving money. If I can learn how to make the stuff, she won't have to spend money to buy any."

Stifling a laugh, Chloe reflected the girl's estimate of her mother's character was dead on. "Go ahead and take your tricorn around back. There's an empty stall next to Trisket," Chloe told her. "I was just about to start my exercises. Afterwards we will eat breakfast, and I'll

show you how to load and clean a pistol. Later we can go down to the river so you can practice with it."

Francis was fascinated by Chloe's exercise routine and peppered the older girl with dozens of questions.

"Why do you do this stuff?" Francis asked.

"It's called Tai Chi," Chloe said. "On the first level it keeps my body limber and relaxes my mind. Higher levels teach a form of self-defense."

"Could you teach it to me?"

Realizing she wasn't going to be able to concentrate enough to reach her center, Chloe agreed to teach the exercises to Francis. Luckily the girl had worn loose fitting trousers and a soft shirt.

"Take off your shoes," Chloe said.

"But the ground will hurt my bare feet," Francis protested.

"It will be okay for today," Chloe said. "Tomorrow I'll see if I can find some of my old practice slippers for you."

The girl proved an apt pupil and soon mastered the beginnings of the exercise. After breakfast Chloe sat Francis down at the table in the library and started having her memorize the parts of the small gun Chloe usually carried, watched by Kimi standing on her hind legs in a chair. The fox seemed to have declared a truce with

Athena who had taken up a place in front of the fire and gone to sleep.

About halfway through the lesson, Giselle quietly laid a small case down on the table in front of Francis.

"You should practice with your own weapon," she said.

"But I don't have one," Francis protested.

Giselle tapped the top of the case. "You do now. Open it."

Slowly Francis lifted the lid. Inside was a small revolver, a cleaning kit and a box of ammunition. Like Chloe's gun, the revolver was meant for a lady's hand. It was an expensive gift; guns, even revolvers like this one, needed each part cast separately and fitted together by hand.

Chloe looked up at Giselle with raised eyebrows.

"I carry a spare," Giselle answered the unspoken question.

"Thank you. I'll pay you for it as soon as I get a job," Francis said.

"Unnecessary," Giselle replied. "You pay us back by helping other women who need it. That is what the Women's Circle was created to do."

"I'll remember," Francis said.

"What are you waiting for?" Chloe

asked. "Take it apart and clean it."

Giselle smiled. She sat down at the table, sipping her coffee.

Kimi stood on her hind legs demanding to be picked up. Chloe lifted the fox into her lap and sat back in her chair watching Francis as she carefully took the revolver apart and cleaned each individual piece.

"Now load it," Chloe instructed. "Remember, leave one cylinder empty and line up the hammer on it, so the gun won't go off if it gets jarred."

As they were about to leave for the firing range, Giselle said, "Francis, I have one more thing for you." She handed the younger girl a leather purse like the one Chloe carried. "All my girls carry these. It may look like a lady's accessory, but it will hold your gun, a knife and a few other defense items we Will explain on your next lesson. For now, put the entire case inside it."

Henry took them down to a place by the river where he had set up three targets. They tied off the tricorns to a hitching rail he had put up.

"We'll be shooting close to the targets because your gun isn't a long-range weapon," he warned Francis. "It's only accurate for about fifteen or twenty feet, so you need to let your opponent get close enough to make your shot count. You first

Chloe, so she can see how it's done."

Chloe drew her pistol and holding it with both hands, she put six shots in the center of the target.

"Now, reload and try it with one hand," he instructed.

This time when she fired, Chloe turned her body sideways and extended her arm straight out from her body. Again, she put six shots in a neat grouping in the bull's eye.

"You hit your target almost every time when you use both hands or your right hand," Henry said. "But it's equally important to be able to fire with your left hand as well. Reload and try it that way."

This time the shots weren't quite in the center of the bull's eye.

"Not bad," Henry told her, "but you need to practice more with your left hand."

He turned to Francis. "Did you see how Chloe stood and how she held her gun?"

Francis nodded.

"Okay, now step up here and take your first shots."

He corrected her stance, telling her to widen the space between her feet, and showed her the two-handed grip Chloe had used.

The gun bucked in her hand when Francis fired it, putting the shots at the edge of the target.

"Not too bad for a first try," Henry told her. "The shots went high because you allowed the kick of the shot to move the barrel of the gun off the target. Don't try to be fast. Shoot slower and try to keep the gun from bucking when you fire. Reload and we'll try it again."

Once the girls had finished, Henry stepped back to twice the distance he had them shooting from and drew his own pistol.

"Why aren't you shooting from the same place we did?" Francis asked.

"Hold up your gun," he told her. He lined his alongside hers. "My gun has a longer barrel which allows for more accuracy at a distance," he said. He handed it to her. "Feel the difference in weight?"

When she nodded, he said, "My gun is heavier because it shoots heavier bullets."

When Francis handed it back to him, he went through the same routine the girls had used.

Caleb woke to the sound of his new cook banging pans in the kitchen. The cooks name was George Carmody. He was a middle-aged man with a bald head who wore a clean white apron over his homespun pants and short-sleeved shirt.

He looked up with a smile when Caleb came downstairs. "Coffee's ready and I've added water to the blue stones in the hot water heater, sir. It should be hot soon if you want a shower before breakfast," he said.

"Thank you, George." Caleb poured himself a cup of coffee to take back upstairs with him.

He was surprised how quickly Junction City had become home. Returning to the kitchen twenty minutes later, he found George had prepared eggs, bacon, gravy and fresh biscuits.

Sitting down at the table, he said, "Please join me. I find a little breakfast conversation goes well with the meal."

George fixed himself a plate and sat down at the table. "Will you be in for lunch?"

"I'm going to be setting up the offices today, so I will be. I'll be out for dinner though."

After breakfast, Caleb went out to the stables to check on the tricorns and the dogs.

His three tricorns were contentedly lipping hay from their morning feed. The dogs were awake, front paws braced on the top of the stall he was using as a

makeshift kennel, pretending they hadn't yet been fed.

"When they've finished, go ahead and let the tricorns out into the corral for some exercise while you muck out the stalls," he told Bill Jenkins, his new Stableman & Kennel Master. "I won't need a mount until this afternoon."

The dogs greeted him happily when he opened the stall. Cernunnos nudged his bowl suggestively.

"How was their appetite this morning?" he asked.

Bill snorted. A tall man with close cropped salt and pepper hair, his common sense had impressed Caleb. When he had watched the man interact with the tricorns and dogs, it was obvious the man liked them. "Voracious, especially him. I had to feed him separately, so he'd let her eat too."

Caleb laughed. "I'll keep them with me in the office to give you time to muck out the stalls. Were your quarters okay?" he asked, referring to the apartment over the stables Bill and George shared.

"Just fine," the man said. "George said it was okay to help myself to the bluestones, so I did. It sure was nice having hot water this morning."

Jim Billing, the man Binns had recommended as a receptionist wandered into the office about nine. Caleb frowned at him. "This office opens at eight. You're late," he said.

"You said the furniture wouldn't be here until ten," Billing replied. He was about medium height which put him several inches below Caleb's six feet. "I didn't figure there was any call to be here before there was a place to sit."

The desks and chairs Caleb had ordered from the carpenter arrived about ten o'clock. Caleb and the delivery men spent the rest of the morning arranging furniture.

The typewriter he had requested arrived as well. He had them place it on Jim's desk.

"What's that for?" Jim eyed the machine as if it was a poisonous snake.

"It's for typing reports and case files," Caleb told him. "There is an instruction manual. I suggest you read it and practice the skill exercises. In your spare time you will be expected to type up the case files in between filing them. I requested three more, but they have to be built by hand apparently, so it will be some time until they arrive."

"I'll be across the street speaking with Sheriff Melody for a while this morning, but I'll be back for lunch. You can take your lunch hour then."

While Caleb and Melody were going over the latest Coroner's report on another dead prostitute, the family at Giselle's house was sitting down to eat lunch.

Afterwards, Francis left, taking her newly cleaned pistol in the purse Giselle had given her.

"I want to try something this afternoon," Chloe told Henry. "I'll need your help."

"What do you plan to do?" he asked.

"I want to talk to the night girls who work the area where the murdered girls found their clients. That's the case Caleb originally came here to help with," she said. "He's been spending all his time helping me search for Adam's killer. It's only fair for me to try and help out with what he originally came here to find out. I'd like you along as backup when I speak to the murdered women's friends. If I'm right, they are more likely to speak freely to me than they did to the Sheriff or his men."

Henry rubbed his chin. "Caleb know about this?"

"He said no, when I told him what I planned," she replied. "He's afraid whoever is killing these girls will fixate on me, because I'm about the right age. They all had dark hair too."

Unhappy at conniving to disobey a

direct prohibition from Caleb, Henry agreed, because he knew if he didn't go along, Chloe would question the girls without him.

"Give me a few minutes to work up a disguise," he said in resignation.

Most of the girls who worked the area where the three dead women had been taken usually set up shop in the late afternoon and worked until the wee hours of the morning.

Chloe rode Trisket through the area first, spotting likely areas where the girls would have enough light for customers to see the wares on display. She spotted a girl alone and stopped in front of her. At Chloe's signal, Athena sat down beside her.

The girl had lank brown hair. Her face showed traces of old powder. The low-cut blouse was sleeveless and the skirt she wore barely reached below her crotch.

She ignored Chloe until she approached her. "I charge extra for women," the prostitute said. "And I don't do dogs."

"I don't want those kinds of services, but I will pay you for your time if you answer a few questions," Chloe told her, allowing a silver chip to show briefly in her hand.

"I ain't no stoolie," the woman said, taking a half step back when Athena

growled at the hostile tone.

"Athena, *Eisteddwich*," Chloe ordered. The dog sat down but continued to keep an eye on the girl.

Chloe smiled. "Ignore Athena; she can be a little over-protective, but She won't jump you unless I say to. I want to ask you about Dorrie, the girl who was murdered. What's your name?"

"I'm Jill. Dorrie ain't around no more," the girl said. "She got herself killed."

"Yes, I know," Chloe said patiently. "Did you see her the day she disappeared?"

Jill shrugged. "Dorrie worked this corner with me sometimes, but I didn't see her the day she disappeared. I overslept so I was late setting up."

Chloe flipped her the silver chip. Jill caught it deftly and bit down on it to test if it was silver.

"This is the real thing," she said, pleased. "No offense but sometimes the Johns try to give us pewter. Is that all you wanted to know?"

Chloe allowed another chip to show. "No. I want to know about the week prior to the day she disappeared. Was anyone watching you girls who wasn't a regular customer?"

Jill gave her a derisive glance. "We get watched all the time by streeters who

don't have money to pay for doing us."

"Did you notice anybody new? Maybe someone who hasn't been back since Dorrie disappeared?"

"Yeah, come to think of it, there was a guy."

"What did he look like?"

Jill shrugged. "Ordinary. Only reason I remember is he gave me the creeps."

"Was he young? Old? In the middle?"

"He wasn't no spring goose, but he wasn't an old man."

"Was he taller than you?"

"Ummn, taller but not much, maybe a head taller than me."

"Thank you." Chloe flipped Jill another two chips and rode on to the next group, where she got about the same information.

When she was satisfied, she signaled Henry she was ready to leave.

"Find out anything interesting?" he asked.

"All the girls remember a middle-aged man who hung around a few days before the last murder," she said. "I'm afraid the description is vague though. He wore good, but not fancy clothing, nothing to mark him out though."

Henry eyed her. "In your questioning the girls did you happen to notice anyone watching you?"

Chloe looked at him, startled. "No, but I wasn't looking particularly. That is why I brought you along. Who did you see?"

"Well there were two men; the first one is a long, tall drink of water with sandy hair and tattoos on his arms. The second man looked an awful lot like Larry Dominique."

"You're sure it was him?"

"Yes," Henry said.

Chloe hesitated, tempted to go back and ask the ladies of the evening if Larry Dominique had been the man they had seen hanging around before Dorrie disappeared, but decided not to do so.

She would mention it to Caleb this evening when he came for dinner.

## IDLE AS A PAINTED SHIP

CALEB CAME BY in the evening with the news he had set up an interview with one of the local Crime bosses.

When he heard Chloe had spent the afternoon questioning the prostitutes, he had a fit.

"Are you crazy woman?" he demanded. "We don't know why he is doing this. What if this killer decides you meet his requirements? You could be making yourself a target."

"Do you want to know what I found out or do you want to yell some more?"

Caleb breathed through his nose, struggling to rein in his temper. It was too late to do anything about her reckless behavior now. "Alright, what did you learn?"

"The girls I talked to said there was middle-aged man watching Dorrie Evans the week before she disappeared. He was neatly dressed, but nothing fancy, and he was shorter than you, probably about five foot eight."

"Something else," Henry put in. "Larry Dominique was hanging around the area. I saw him."

"Did he follow you there or was he already there when you arrived?"

"He was already there. He was standing

in the shade next to Grover's feed store."

"Did any of the girls name him as this mysterious watcher?"

"I didn't get a chance to ask them," Chloe said. "I only realized he had been there when Henry mentioned it on the way home."

"He's such a meek little man," Giselle protested. "I have a hard time imagining him as a killer of women. Why his wife walks all over him."

"Anyone can snap," Henry reminded her. "Maybe he got tired of her ordering him around, but he doesn't have the nerve to go after her."

"So you think the prostitutes are a substitute for Cora?" Giselle asked.

"Aren't we jumping to conclusions here? He's a bookkeeper," Chloe pointed out. "Maybe he does the books for the feed store and he was outside taking a break."

"It's possible; the men I talked to on the docks say Dominique does work there, but not full time. I'll pass the information along to Melody," Caleb said. "He can run with it. Until we know one way or another about Dominique, please don't go back there Chloe."

"I was just trying to help," she said. Seeing the real worry in his eyes, she gave in. "Alright, I won't go back and ask if they know him. You have to admit, I got more information than you and the Sheriff did, though."

"Yes, you did. You helped," he said. Hoping to divert her, he added "I've arranged for us to meet with one of the local crime Chief's tomorrow. I'll pick you up in the evening about ten o'clock."

"Was it hard to set up a meeting?" Chloe asked him.

"No," he said. "It was surprisingly easy, and that worries me somewhat."

"Do you think it's a trap?"

"It doesn't feel that way," he admitted. "But—"

"I thought us ladies were the only ones who decided things based on feelings," Chloe teased.

He scowled. "Shut up. My intuition has kept me alive more than once, so I pay attention to it. Are you sure I can't talk you out of going with me?"

Henry laughed. "You're wasting your time, boy. She's as stubborn as the rest of her sex. Besides, if she's going to become an Enforcer, she can't back away from something like this."

Caleb had hired a carriage to take them to the meeting. Chloe was not surprised to find Henry sitting on the Dickey Box in the driver's place.

"I see you decided to take a few precautions after all," she said.

Henry snorted. "Get inside girl and let's get this over with."

The meeting took place at a warehouse near the docks. Caleb swung down from the carriage door and walked over to the two men lounging beside a large docking area.

"He's expecting us," he said.

The larger of the two men nodded. "You're Jones?"

"Yes, and this is Miss DeMille. The driver's name is Henry. He'll wait outside with the carriage."

"Okay," he said. "I'm Tim. Follow me."

He turned and walked into the darkened interior of the warehouse.

"Doesn't your boss believe in lights?" Chloe asked after she had accidentally kicked over a small wooden crate.

"The less you see, the better it will be for you," Tim retorted.

He led them into a comfortable room in the warehouse's rear. To Chloe's relief, it had decent lighting. It resembled a well-off businessman's den, with its floor to ceiling lined bookshelves, cozy chairs and writing tables.

"Jones and DeMille are here, boss," Tim said laconically.

Chloe stopped and stared. The man facing them in the overstuffed chair behind the massive desk was plainly related to Caleb. Like Caleb he was dark

with knife edged features. Unlike Caleb
though, there was a devilish twinkle in
this man's eyes, as though he enjoyed the
joke life had played on him.

"Well, now. So this is where you ended
up," Caleb remarked.

The man grinned. "That's right, cousin.
I got tired of taking orders from fools,
so I became my own boss."

"Chloe, this is my cousin Hercule
Jones," Caleb said. "Hercule, this is my
partner, Enforcer Chloe DeMille."

"Pleased to meet you, Ma'am," Hercule
said, making no effort to rise from his
chair.

"Well, this certainly answers the
question of why it was so easy to obtain
an interview," Chloe told Caleb.

"So it would seem." Caleb took a seat
in one of the other chairs, motioning for
Chloe to do the same.

"How can I help you cousin?" Hercule
asked.

"How much can you tell us about a
shopkeeper named Samuel Adams?"

Hercule shrugged. "Not a lot. He was a
small-time fence. He paid his protection
fee the same as the others."

"He was something of a lady's man,"
Chloe said. "Did he make any enemies?"

"Nobody who would want to kill him; at
least not anyone I know of."

"And you would know if someone from your sphere of influence killed him, wouldn't you?"

"I'd better know," his cousin said. "Any terminations around here by any of my people could only happen if I gave permission, and I haven't given it."

"You aren't the only boss around here though. Would you hear if any of your competitors had him taken out?"

"Yes, If one of us does something, we usually all get to hear about it."

"Did he work for you?"

"I wouldn't say worked exactly; he paid a percentage of whatever he fenced to me. His operation wasn't big enough to hurt me if he got taken out."

"Any enemies who might want to put the blame on you for his murder?"

His cousin flashed him a quick glance. "There have been some ruffles in the power fabric of Junction City lately. A new boss is moving in on the rackets."

"Got a name?"

"Sorry, only an alias. He calls himself the Big Man. I will have his real name soon."

"Okay. When you get a name please pass it on."

Hercule grinned. "Anything for family."

"Were you aware there's been a rash of killings of street people in the past few

weeks?"

"I'm looking into it," Hercule replied.

"Who do you think is doing it?"

"No idea. Yet." Hercule's voice was iron. "But two of the women had paid me for protection. When I find out who did this, I'll take care of it myself."

Caleb shook his head. "Why do it yourself when the law will take care of it?"

"Come now," Hercule said with a grin, "They were under my protection. If I don't take care of it, word might get out I can't do what I'm being paid for."

Caleb let it go, asking instead, "Do you think the killings have anything do with the power struggle you mentioned?"

"Maybe. I'm checking into it."

"It would be cleaner if you turned what you know over to me and let the law handle punishment for the deaths," Chloe suggested.

He shook his head. "I can't do that."

"Moving on," Caleb Said, "What do you know about a photographer named Jeffrey Doimer?"

Hercule laughed. "Is that what she's calling herself now?"

"You know he's a woman?" Chloe asked.

"He grew up here. My people tell me sometime in his early teens, Doimer decided he didn't like the job

opportunities open to women in my world, so he started dressing like a boy. He got his start as a photographer from old Doimer, the man who used to take pictures for the Junction City Herald. That's when he changed his name. When the old man died, he inherited his equipment."

"Did he kill him?" Caleb asked and Chloe shot him a quick look of surprise, but she kept her inevitable questions to herself.

"I don't know. Way I heard it the old man died in bed."

"All right. Thank you for your help, Hercule," Caleb stood up and Chloe did too.

Hercule rapped on the floor with an ornate cane leaning against the desk, and Tim came to the door. "See my cousin and his partner out, please," Hercule said.

Tim led them back through the darkened warehouse. Henry was still sitting on the dickey box, tensely watching the door. He relaxed when Caleb and Chloe came out.

Once the carriage had started back to Giselle's house, Chloe looked across the darkened interior at Caleb.

"Why did you ask if Doimer had killed his mentor?" She asked.

"Doimer is a man who has an eye to the main chance," he said. "Once the old man had taught him his trade and introduced

him to his contacts in the newspaper, he would have been no more use to Doimer. It makes sense to ask if he got rid of him."

Chloe suppressed a shiver. "I suppose so. It just seems so—heartless somehow."

"Doimer didn't strike me as someone with much of a heart," Caleb said dryly.

"Did you know your cousin was here in Junction City before you came?" She asked.

Caleb hesitated. He was going to lie, Chloe thought with a sinking feeling.

"I knew he had escaped from Copper City, the same as I had," Caleb said. "If we lost the war, we all had standing orders not to try and track each other in case we led our enemies to a family member."

Not a lie but he hadn't exactly answered the question either, she thought.

Caleb was at the house in time for breakfast the next morning. Chloe eyed him thoughtfully. She considered making a snarky remark about it but changed her mind. It wasn't as if they didn't have plenty of food to spare. He probably hadn't had time to arrange for meals wherever he was living, she told herself.

"I came to touch bases, so I'd know what your plans for the day are," he said.

"That is a good idea. Why don't you start first?" Chloe asked.

"I'm going down to the docks to check the ship's manifests. I want to find out

who had just arrived before each of the prostitute murders. Maybe I can get a line on who we should be investigating."

"Didn't Sheriff Melody do it already?" Henry asked.

"He checked the arrivals *after* the murders. I'm working on a theory the murderer picked his targets. If so, he would need to be in the area before he chose a girl."

"I've got deliveries to make," Chloe said. "While I'm downtown, I plan to talk to Mary Jessup again."

"You'll take Athena with you?" Caleb asked.

"Yes," Chloe said resignedly. "I'll take her."

## BRIGHT AS A NEW PENNY

A SHORT, terse note from Grace Trevelyan had arrived the day before asking for a progress report on the investigation had reminded Chloe she still needed to do a follow up interview with Mary Jessup.

She was going to be in the area to make deliveries, anyway, so today would be a good time to ask Mary the questions she wanted answered.

After making her deliveries and taking a few new orders, Chloe stepped outside onto the boardwalk. Adams Mercantile had reopened and the Law Enforcement Official seal had been removed, she realized. Obviously, Grace and Marissa had found someone to run the store since Marissa was still under a doctor's care and Grace too busy with council business to be there full time. Several other shopkeepers were out on the sidewalks attending to various chores.

She spotted the younger Mrs. Jessup pushing her baby in a stroller along the boardwalk. She hoped Mary Jessup would talk a lot more freely today than she had in front of her mother-in-law.

Although dismay showed in her face when she recognized Chloe, Mary pulled herself together. In answer to Chloe's question about how well she knew Adams, she

admitted, "I sort of dated him a little; we met for coffee a couple of times. I thought he was handsome and dangerous. I knew he was married, but he claimed it was just a convenience and I found him attractive enough to believe it. He said he had wanted the store and his wife owned a half interest in it. When they got married, he talked her and her sister into letting him run it."

"When did you decide you didn't like him?" Chloe asked, watching the girl's face.

Mary flushed. "I may have found him fascinating, but I wouldn't let him touch me unless we were married. I thought he understood and respected that, but—"

"He forced you, didn't he?"

Mary gave her a shamefaced look. "How did you know?"

"Because he did the same thing to a couple of other women." Chloe eyed her shrewdly. "Is the baby his?"

"No!" Mary said passionately. "But I was late with my period and I got scared. The next time Jase asked me to marry him, I agreed if we could do it as soon as possible."

Chloe looked down at the peacefully sleeping little boy. "I believe you; he looks too big for a seven-month child."

"Davy was born nine months after we got

married," Mary told her fiercely.

"Did Adams keep pestering you after you got married?"

"Yes," she whispered. "He threatened to tell Jase we were having an affair and that Davy was his."

"What did you do about his threat?"

"I told Jase Adams was still chasing me, and I didn't go anywhere alone unless there was a lot of people around. Jase said he'd take care of it and I wasn't to worry."

"What did he plan to do about it?"

"I don't know. I think he intended to beat him up or something."

"There are a lot of places you could take Davy on a walk. Why take him here where Adams could see you?"

"I wanted to prove I wasn't afraid of him," Mary said.

"Do you ever use poison to get rid of rats Mary?" she asked, switching tactics.

The girl shuddered. "No, I hate them, but I'm afraid of poison."

"Does your mother-in-law?"

"Well, yes, but I told her she had to lock it up somewhere and asked her not to use it while Davy is crawling around."

"Where did she put it?"

"Out in the garden shed, I think. Why?"

"Because Adams was poisoned. He was only stabbed after he died."

Mary turned white. "I didn't! I didn't kill him!" She ducked her head and turned the stroller around. "I'm sorry, I can't talk anymore."

Chloe watched her retreat in silence. Mary had given her a lot of things to think about. She collected Trisket from the hitching rail and rode toward the Cafe where Caleb said to meet him.

## THE DEATH FIRES DANCE

WHILE CHLOE and Caleb were pursuing their investigations into the two separate crimes, another type of pursuit was taking place. Levi Judson hadn't liked being humiliated by a woman at the dance. He was furious with Chloe and had determined to be revenged on her later. When he realized Cora Dominique had held back one of the jewels, his rage transferred to her.

It was easy enough for him to find out the address of the house rented by Larry Dominique and he headed over there. He wasn't too worried about Dominique; the man had been brave enough when he'd had the backing of the Enforcer, but on his own he seemed too meek to put up much opposition.

Francis had just returned from her third lesson when she heard the commotion downstairs.

She stopped on the landing to listen, realizing from Judson's accusation that her mother must have kept one of the jewels Judson had paid her instead of giving them all to her husband so he could return them. Now Judson was demanding Lila service him as if she were a whore. Francis's mouth thinned. If her mother had kept one of the jewels, she would have hidden it in the secret compartment in her jewelry box.

Cora's jewelry box had a hidden partition; Francis had discovered it when she was Sydney's age.

"What's going on?" her younger sister Hetty asked her. She and Sydney were standing in the doorway of the room they shared. Both of them looked frightened.

They could all hear Lila sobbing downstairs. The sick fear roiling inside Francis ever since the dance came to a boil.

"Trouble," she told the younger girls. "Go down to the stable and stay with the tricorns. I'll come get you when it's safe."

Not waiting to see if the girls obeyed her, Francis went along to her mother's room. The jewel, a large, square-cut emerald, winked up at her from the hidden compartment. She pushed her mother's diary aside and stuffed the jewel into her pocket.

She was still wearing the leather purse Giselle had given her. She slipped her hand into it and drew out the small pistol. Holding the gun down beside her leg, she went downstairs.

Lila was cowering against the wall, and Cora Dominique was facing Judson with her hands on her hips. "I consider that jewel a dowry payment," she told him defiantly. "You don't touch my daughter until after the wedding!"

"That's going to be a little difficult," Francis said quietly. "I understand Mr. Judson is already married."

"Are you already married?" Cora demanded.

"What difference does it make you old witch?" Judson asked. "I paid to pop her cherry." He turned on Lila, "Get upstairs and wait for me. Put on a pretty nightie; I like ripping them off."

With a gasp of fear, Lila dodged around Francis and ran up the stairs.

Francis placed herself between Judson and the stairs. "You want your jewel back?" she asked. She took it out of her pocket and threw it at him. "Here, take it and get out."

The stone bounced off his nose, leaving a shallow cut bleeding sluggishly. Judson's eyes narrowed in rage.

"How dare you?" Cora screeched at her daughter. "You thief! You stole that out of my jewelry box! I'll whip you for this!"

"Shut up Mother," Francis said, not taking her eyes off Judson. The man's face had turned beet red and a snarl curled his mouth.

"Yes, Cora," Larry Dominique said from the kitchen doorway, "shut your mouth. You've got all your jewels back Judson. Please leave."

Judson laughed. "Or what? You think you can stop me, you little worm? I'll teach you not to interfere with your betters."

Judson drew his knife and circled her father who gave a high shrill laugh. To Francis's shock, Larry Dominique drew a knife as well.

Her father's laugh sent a chill down Francis's spine. When she looked at the man who sired her, she could see the unholy excitement in his eyes.

Cora screamed, watching in horror as her plans crumbled before her eyes.

As the two men fought, Francis backed slowly up the stairs.

Judson had been sure of winning the knife battle. To his astonishment, the man he had despised as weak, ruthlessly cut him to pieces with the knife. He died in a pool of blood on Cora's pristine floor.

Oblivious to her own danger Cora accused her husband, "You've ruined everything!"

"Shut up Cora," a note of unhealthy excitement in his voice, Larry turned on her, the bloody knife still in his hand.

"You put that away, Larry," Cora ordered, but she backed away from his advance.

"Why don't you scream for me, dear," Dominique said, and giggled.

Terrified at what she was sure was

about to happen, Francis turned and ran up the stair, colliding with Lila on the landing. Realizing the sobbing Lila was incapable of independent action, Francis grabbed her sister's hand and pulled her down the back stairs toward the stable. Behind them she heard her mother's screams cut off by a gurgle.

Down at the stable, there was no sign of the man they had employed to care for the animals, but Hetty had managed to saddle both tricorns.

"Get on," Francis told her. "Lila will ride behind you. She's in no state to control a tricorn."

Once she had Lila up behind Hetty, she mounted the other tricorn. She slipped her foot out of the stirrup and rode the animal over to the mounting block. "Sydney, come and get on behind me," she said.

"Where will we go?" Hetty asked.

"We're going to see Giselle St. Vyr," Francis said. "She and Chloe will know what we need to do next."

"Did that man kill Momma and Poppa?" Sydney asked.

"No, but I think Mother is dead or at least badly hurt. She and Father were fighting when I left, and he was very angry."

"Shouldn't we have tried to help her?" Hetty asked.

Francis shook her head. "I'll go back after I get you girls to a safe place."

The two younger girls were silent for the rest of the ride to Giselle's house. Lila was apparently frozen in shock. Francis realized her sister must have seen at least a portion of the fight when her father killed Judson and turned on his wife.

If their father had killed their mother, they were now alone in the world. Francis knew the responsibility of taking care of Hetty and Sydney was going to fall on her, and she wasn't prepared; she would need to find a job, a place for them to live, and see the two younger girls finished their education. Lila would be useless; in fact Francis was probably going to need to take care of her as well.

When Francis brought her small party into Giselle's parlor, the older woman took one look at their faces and held out her arms.

Francis burst into overwrought tears on her shoulder.

"I didn't know where else to come," she gasped out. "He killed him, and I think he killed her too."

"Mrs. Syms, take the younger girls out into the kitchen and fix them some cookies and milk," Giselle asked. "You can have Mary bring us a pot of tea in here.

Afterwards she needs to prepare the spare bedrooms for guests."

Once Mrs. Syms had bustled Hetty and Sydney out to the kitchen, Giselle turned to Francis.

"Now what happened?"

"Judson came to the house. He said Mother had kept some of the jewels he had paid her for Lila. He demanded Lila have sex with him then and there. I knew where Mother would have put any jewels she wanted to hide, so I found it and brought it downstairs. Mother and Judson were fighting about it. She said he had to marry Lila before he could use her. I told Mother you had said he was married already and threw the jewel at him. Mother started screaming I was a thief. Then Father arrived. Judson pulled a knife and so did father. They started to fight."

"Is your father dead?"

Francis took a deep breath. "No, he killed Judson, afterwards I think he turned on Mother. He—there was something wrong with him. He scared me so badly, all I could think of was I had to get my sisters out of there. I didn't know where else to come."

"You did exactly what you should have done," Giselle said. She glanced over at Lila who was rocking herself back and forth with her arms hugged around her

body.

"What's wrong with her?"

"I don't know. I think she must have seen part of the fight. She was on the landing when I ran upstairs to get away. She's always been easily frightened."

"She might be in shock. We'll put her to bed in one of the spare rooms and send for the doctor. I'm sorry, but we only have two extra rooms, you'll have to share with her."

Francis nodded. "That's alright. If Mother is dead, I'm going to have to find a way to take care of them all now."

"Well, we'll make those plans tomorrow," Giselle said. "In the meantime, I'll send a message to Caleb so he and Chloe can check out what shape your parents are in. Come child, even if you are correct in thinking your father killed your mother, you aren't alone; you have me and Chloe as well as the rest of the Women's Circle to help you."

# DEAD MEN'S TALES

AS AGREED, Caleb and Chloe met at the same coffee shop they had used before. Chloe and Athena arrived first. After letting Trisket stick her nose into the water trough, Chloe went inside, selecting a table allowing her to watch the street outside. The waitress, a young girl about eighteen with her hair tied back in a neat braid, eyed Athena warily, but when the dog laid down beside Chloe, she decided to ignore her.

"What can I get for you today, Miss?" she asked.

"Two cups, a small pot of coffee and some cream and sugar please," Chloe told her with a smile.

"Are you expecting your gentleman friend?" the girl asked.

"Yes, he should be here shortly," Chloe said.

"Gentlemen are always hungry, we have some tasty small sandwiches on special today," the waitress suggested.

"Thank you, I expect he will like that," Chloe said.

When the girl came back with a tray, she set the coffee pot over a small bluestone warmer and poured a small amount of water over the pebbles. The stones lit a small flame which would keep the pot

warm. She set the cups, a pitcher of cream and a sugar bowl on the table, along with silverware, two small plates and a tiered serving stand of prettily made sandwiches.

When Caleb arrived, he left the two dogs who had accompanied him lying in the shade by the hitching rail.

"Bless you!" he said as he came to sit down. "I've been wanting a cup of good coffee for the past hour. The stuff the Sheriff serves tastes like burnt mud."

He reached down and patted Athena who had sat up and nudged him with her nose. "Good girl," he told her. "Lie back down now."

"Did you get a chance to speak to Mary?" he asked.

Holding the cup with both hands, Chloe sipped her coffee. Absently, she picked up one of the tiny sandwiches and held it out to Athena who took it delicately and before she swallowed it whole.

"I'm afraid we can't rule her out," she said. "Adams was trying to blackmail her into having sex with him; he threatened to tell Jase Davy was his child."

"That ties in a little with what Jessup told me; he knew Adams was chasing Mary. He claimed she was afraid of him."

"It might be true," Chloe said slowly, "but Mary deliberately walked past Adams Mercantile whenever she took Davy out in

the stroller, and her mother-in-law keeps poison around for the rats. According to Mary it's kept in the garden shed, but I'm not satisfied she couldn't have gotten hold of some."

"How did she get it into Adams?" Caleb asked.

"The sheriff's men tested the half-open whiskey bottle in the storeroom. It had a pretty good-sized dose of the stuff"

"She would have needed to sneak into the store when neither Adams or his wife were home to add it to his liquor," Caleb pointed out. "She strikes me as too timid to do that, besides I don't think she is capable of the kind of planning it would need to carry it out."

"I know. I don't think so either. Did you find out anything useful from her husband?"

"No. He claims he was at baseball practice the night Adams was killed. He said Mary and his parents watched from the stands."

"Did he know—"

She broke off because Mrs. Syms son Tomas threw open the door to the coffee shop.

"Miss Chloe," he gasped out. "Thank God I found you. Mrs. St. Vyr says for you to get over to the Dominique residence as fast as you can. You too sir."

"Slow down, Tomas," Chloe said. "Why does she want us to go there?"

Tomas took a deep breath. "Miss Francis brought her sisters to the house. She was babbling something about somebody getting killed."

"Do you know where we're going?" Caleb asked. "I've never been there."

"Yes, Francis gave me the address. Do you want to bring Sheriff Melody in on this?"

Caleb shrugged. "It's his town. We have to notify him." He turned to Tomas, "Do you know how to get to the Sheriff's office?"

Tomas nodded.

"Alright, as soon as you catch your breath, ride over to Melody and tell him what you just told us. Tell him we'll meet him there."

Caleb stood up and dropped a silver chip on the table, telling the waitress the extra was for her.

Chloe smelled the coppery scent of old blood as soon as she walked in the door of the Dominique residence. They found Judson's body in the hallway. A long fighting blade had fallen near his hand. His body had been sliced open, and a path of drying blood still coated his neck and trailed onto the floor.

A little further into the house Chloe

spotted a blood-soaked blue linen dress. Inside it was the remains of Cora Dominique. The woman's body had literally been sliced into ribbons. There was a lot of blood. Arterial spray from where her throat had been cut splashed up the walls.

Knowing it was useless, she knelt by Cora and checked her pulse.

"It's no use," Caleb said. "They're both dead Chloe."

She sighed. "I know, I just had to check."

"Two bodies mean there had to be a third person here. We need to search the house."

He looked over at her. "Have you ever cleared a crime scene?"

"No, but I know how it's done," she replied. "We stick together and check each room, right?"

"Yes," he said.

The house was empty. Bloody footprints led out the back door towards the stable.

Sheriff Melody wasn't happy when he saw the bodies.

"Miss DeMille, you know the family. When did the Dominiques get to Junction City?" he asked.

"They arrived on the Saucy Sue the same as we did," she told him. "Giselle, Lizette and I shared a cabin with Cora Dominique and her daughters."

"Did the husband travel with them?"

Chloe frowned. "I don't remember seeing him at meals or on the deck. He was there when the boat docked."

"Why do you want to know?" Caleb asked.

"You didn't see the dead prostitutes' bodies," Melody said. "The wounds on these bodies look like the same weapon."

Caleb frowned. "I thought the first woman was killed several weeks ago."

Melody scowled. "She was. I was hoping we might have a match. But if Dominique didn't get here until three weeks ago, he can't be our man."

"He didn't travel with us from Junction City," Chloe said. "He met the boat when we docked."

"So he was already in town?" Melody asked.

"I suppose so," she said. "I think Francis said he had come ahead of them to look for work. He's a bookkeeper you know."

"Sheriff, is it okay for me to pack some clothes for the girls? I'm pretty sure they ran off without anything."

Melody hesitated. "Okay, just let one of my men look through anything you take."

She nodded and went upstairs to pack some necessities for Francis and her sisters. At the last minute, she dropped Cora Dominique's jewelry box into the satchel with the girls' clothes.

"Probably a good thing to take it with you. It wouldn't do to leave it here where it might get stolen," Melody said when his deputy showed it to him.

Jeffrey Doimer showed up to take crime scene pictures while Chloe and Caleb were tying satchels with spare clothing for the girls on their tricorns. He carefully avoided catching Chloe's eye, choosing instead to report to the deputy Melody was leaving in charge while he went to question the Dominique girls.

Melody accompanied Caleb and Chloe back to Giselle's house.

"Is Miss Dominique available to talk to?" he asked Giselle.

"Which one?" she asked. "We put Lila to bed as she seems to be in shock. I imagine she will be able to talk in the morning."

"I can tell you what I saw," Francis said quietly from the stairs. "I sent my little sisters out to the stable before any real fighting started. They are in bed also, but you can speak to them tomorrow."

Melody nodded.

"Come into the parlor dear," Giselle said. "You can speak privately there."

When Francis was seated, she looked Melody in the eye. "Is my Mother dead?"

"Yes," he replied.

"I would appreciate it if you allowed me to tell my sisters before you speak to

them tomorrow."

"I reckon that's only natural," Melody agreed. "We also found the body of Levi Judson in your house. Do you know who killed him or your mother?"

Francis took a deep breath. "No, not for sure. The only other person there was my Father. I think he killed Judson with a knife. I was frightened, so I ran upstairs to get away. I found Lila on the landing and I pulled her with me when I ran to the stables."

"So when you left, there was no one in the house but your Father, your Mother and Judson?"

"Yes."

Melody studied the girl thoughtfully. She appeared calm and collected, but he had experience with women who seemed composed and later dissolved into a weeping mess. His next question was a tricky one; if she got defensive of her father, she could either weep or turn into a spitfire; he didn't like either possibility, but He decided to chance it anyway.

"If your father wanted to hide out, where would he go?"

"Why would he hide? Oh, you think he killed Judson, don't you?"

"He might have. Judson had friends, maybe your dad is hiding from them."

Melody had carefully not mentioned the possibility Larry Dominique had murdered his wife Cora. Chloe's eyebrows rose, and she exchanged a glance with Caleb seeing a matching comprehension in his eyes.

"I don't know," Francis said. "Mother didn't like his friends so he didn't bring them to the house."

Lila was better the next morning, but she got hysterical when Francis told her Sheriff Melody wanted to talk to her about what she had seen at the house.

Resisting the urge to slap the girl sharply, Chloe made some soothing tea and had Mary take her back to bed.

The two younger girls had sat wide eyed and silent when Francis told them their mother was dead.

"What's going to happen now?" Hetty asked.

"I'm going to take care of you," Francis told her. "I'll get a job to support us."

"And in the meantime," Giselle intervened, "the four of you will stay here with me and Chloe."

"Thank you," Francis said. "I know it's an imposition. As soon as I get a job, I'll pay you room and board for us—"

"Don't be silly girl," Giselle said. "I'll enjoy having young things in the house again."

"What about Lila?" Chloe asked. "Shouldn't we have a doctor look at her? She can't keep having these hysterical fits and hiding in her bed."

"I'm sorry she's being so much trouble," Francis said stiffly.

"Don't you start," Chloe pointed a finger at her. "This isn't about taking advantage of our hospitality, it's about her mental health."

Francis held up her hands in surrender. "Got it."

Caleb and Sheriff Melody went to see Francis again before they started their search for Dominique.

"He hasn't contacted us," she told them when they asked about her father.

"Is your sister feeling well enough to speak to us?" Melody asked.

"The doctor is with her now," Francis said. "She got hysterical this morning at breakfast when I mentioned giving you a statement."

Caleb studied her thoughtfully. "You're sure you didn't see any more than you told us?"

"I'm sorry, my back was to the room when I ran up the stairs."

Doctor Sanderson and Giselle entered the room.

"How is your patient Doctor? Is she well enough to speak to us?"

"No," Sanderson said, "and frankly, I doubt if she ever will be. She says she doesn't remember anything about yesterday."

"Is she telling the truth?"

"Hysterical amnesia isn't unusual in cases like this. It might be the shock of whatever she saw was so great her mind has blocked it out."

"I see," Melody said.

"Is she going to need nursing Doctor?" Francis asked.

"I don't think so. There isn't anything physically wrong with her you know."

"Do you think it would be alright if I left her with my younger sisters when I go to work?"

"It should be fine," he assured her. "What kind of work do you do?"

"I don't know what I'll be doing," Francis answered. "But I need to find a job. Mother had an allowance from her family, but I don't know if the payments will continue so I need to be able to provide for my sisters. Hetty and Sydney are too young, and they need to finish their schooling. Lila—well she doesn't know how to do anything to would earn her way."

"You're going to be looking for Larry Dominique, aren't you?" Chloe asked from the doorway.

"Yes," he admitted. "I'll be assisting the Sheriff. What are your plans for today?"

Chloe held up an envelope. "This just came. It's from Susan Fisher, she wants to see me."

"Don't go alone," he said, "and take Athena with you."

"I'll go with her," Giselle volunteered. "It's been some time since I did something interesting like this."

## HOLD OFF! UNHAND ME!

THE INTERVIEW with Susan Fisher was unproductive; Chloe introduced Giselle and the three of them made small talk for a few minutes.

Realizing the woman wouldn't come to the point unless she was prodded into it, Chloe said, "Your note said you had remembered something you thought might help us."

"Oh, well, I don't like to spread gossip."

"It isn't gossip if it pertains to a man's murder," Chloe said.

"I think Samuel was having an affair with the new photographer woman."

"I see. Thank you, but we already know about it."

Susan Fisher rose. "Oh, dear look at the time! I hate to cut your visit short, but I'm due at a committee meeting and I need to change my shoes."

"Here's your hat, what's your hurry," Giselle remarked, and Chloe laughed as the door shut behind them.

"Where's our driver?" Chloe remarked when she saw the rickshaw they had rented was unattended.

"He seems to have disappeared," Chloe said.

The warning growl from Athena barely

had time to register when a man grabbed her around the waist from behind, attempting to force a foul-smelling cloth over her nose and mouth. When she kicked back at him, he simply lifted her off the ground so her feet couldn't get purchase. She fought fiercely, stabbing back at her captor's eyes with her hands.

Another man had grabbed Giselle and was attempting to do the same to her. When he saw Athena's deadly rush, he dropped the rag and pulled a gun, firing quickly. The shot clipped the dog's head and she went down.

Her captor had succeeded in forcing the cloth over Chloe's nose and mouth and the world went black.

Chloe woke with a bad taste in her mouth. It was hard to breathe. When she turned her head the air got cleaner. She discovered she was face down in the dirt. When she tried to push herself upright, she realized her hands were bound in front of her and pinned under her body.

With some effort, she turned on her side allowing her arms to bend at the elbow. She rolled onto her back and used her bound hands to grip her knees pulling herself upright. At least they hadn't tied her feet.

Blinking dirt out of her eyes she looked around. She was in a room with a dirt floor. The slats making up the walls were warped, allowing some light to filter through them. A narrow, barred window allowed her to realize it was dark outside. How long had she been here? How had she been taken?

She heard a small sound from across the room. It came from a barely seen lump next to the other wall. Giselle! Giselle had been with her. Using the wall to pull herself upright, Chloe stood unsteadily on her feet. With one hand on the wall, she staggered over to the older woman.

"Giselle!" she said, the words coming out as a croak. "Giselle can you hear me. Roll over on your back."

Giselle coughed. Still holding onto the wall for support, Chloe knelt beside her friend and rolled the other woman over on her back. She brushed dirt off Giselle's face, frowning when her hand brushed something crusty. A fragment of it clung to her fingers. She brought them to her mouth and tested them with her tongue. Blood. What she had taken for dirt was dried blood. Carefully she ran a hand over Giselle's face and head. There was a goose egg lump just above her temple. Their captives must have hit her.

Chloe needed her hands free. She reached into the top of her boot for the small knife she always carried there.

Obviously, whoever had taken them hadn't done a thorough job searching them for weapons. She pulled the knife out of the specially made leather sheath in the boot. Holding it awkwardly, she managed to insert the blade under the ropes tying her hands. She bit down on the hilt, using her teeth to hold the knife securely and rubbed her hands up and down. The knife was sharp. It quickly cut through the ropes around her hands.

Once her hands had regained some feeling, she fumbled around for Giselle's bonds and cut them as well.

Giselle was still unconscious, but she was breathing easier now that her face was out of the dirt.

Chloe stood up and went to the barred window to look out. It was difficult because the opening was over her head. Gripping the bars, she pulled herself up so she could see out. The moon was up. There was nothing to tell her where she was. From the window she could see the moon shining on the river. It was quiet except for the small rustles of animals and the far-off hoot of a night hunting bird.

They must have been taken out of the city. She groped her way around the room until she found the door. When she pushed on it, she realized it had been barred on the outside. The door didn't fit well; she could see the outside bar through the door jamb. It might be possible to move the bar with her knife, but it would have to wait until Giselle woke up or daylight, whichever came first.

She was sure Caleb and Henry would be searching for them. She would have to apologize to Caleb for Athena's death. When the two men had grabbed her, she remembered seeing the huge dog charging toward them. The man struggling with Giselle had clipped her on the head with his pistol and fired at the dog just as she leaped at him. Athena had gone down on top of the man, who pushed her body off himself before rising. Despite her struggles, Chloe's captor had succeeded in holding a chloroform rag over her face and the world had gone dark.

She and Giselle had gone to Susan Fisher's house at the woman's request. They hadn't learned much from her. The woman had been nervous. She had asked them questions about what the Sheriff and Caleb knew about Adams death.

It was when they were leaving that the two men had grabbed them. For some reason, the men had looked familiar. The memory teased her, but she couldn't bring it out in the open.

Frustrated, she sat down and lifted

Giselle's head into her lap.

Giselle was beginning to stir when Chloe saw faint fingers of light were filtering through the window bars.

"My head hurts," Giselle said. "Is there any water?"

"I'm afraid not," Chloe replied. "How much do you remember?"

"Mrs. Fisher was a trap," Giselle said grimly. "Those two men were waiting in her driveway when we left. Where are we?"

"Somewhere out in the delta," Chloe told her. "I couldn't see much out the window in the dark. Now it's light I can try again."

Giselle sat up. "We need to get out of here."

"I agree," Chloe retorted. "I think I can—"

"Sssh! Someone's coming," Giselle whispered.

Both women could hear the trotting tricorns pulling up outside.

"Watch him, he's tricky, Tim," a voice said.

"Not tied up like a bird for dressing," another voice retorted.

Chloe tensed. She heard the bar being lifted before a man was roughly shoved inside. His hands were bound but his feet were free, he spun and aimed a kick at the big man in the door.

He hit him, but he was off balance and staggered. The second man drew his pistol and cocked it.

"Back off," he said. "The boss said to take you alive, but I don't have to kill you to stop you."

"Caleb?" Giselle asked, staring.

"Oh, so you're awake, are you?" Tim said, picking himself up off the ground.

"He isn't Caleb, Giselle," Chloe said. "Allow me to introduce his cousin Hercule to you."

The other man continued to hold a pistol on them while Tim threw in a canvas sack. "Food and Water. I suggest you use it. You're going to be here a while until the boss decides what to do with you."

He slammed the door closed and they all heard the bar being dropped.

Hercule executed a small bow. "Ladies," he said.

Chloe retrieved her knife from her boot sheath and said, "Hold out your hands so I can get those ropes off."

Giselle had picked up the canvas bag and was unpacking the food and water skin.

"Well," she said. "At least they aren't going to starve us."

Chloe stepped back and sheathed her knife. "Weren't those the two men guarding you the night we met?"

He scowled at her. "Yes," he admitted.

"I seem to have slipped up."

"Why did they take you?"

"I told you and Caleb there was a power struggle going on. The new man apparently decided I know too much. He bribed my men to betray me."

Giselle had taken a drink from the waterskin and handed it to Chloe. She divided the smoked meat and hard cheese loaf into three portions.

"Is this the crime boss you met?" she asked.

"Yes," Chloe replied. "Apparently he is also Caleb's cousin."

"What are you two doing here?" Hercule asked. "I find it hard to believe the pair of you could be a threat to the self-styled Big Man. It's what he calls himself."

"Did you find out more about him?" Chloe asked.

Hercule snorted. "I must have been closer than I thought, but damned if I can figure out what triggered this."

"He must have some connection to the Fishers, or at least to Susan Fisher," Giselle remarked. "It was from her house they took us."

"And she asked us to come to her," Chloe added. She looked over at Giselle consideringly. "You don't suppose—"

"It wouldn't be the first time a government official turned out to be involved in organized crime," Giselle agreed.

Chloe was looking through a crack in the wall. "I don't believe it—they're riding off."

"What?" exclaimed Hercule. He went to look out the window. "It's just plain stupid. Leaving us here without a guard of some type?"

"They left Giselle and me alone here last night. If Giselle hadn't been unconscious, we would have been gone when you got here today."

"How do you intend to get out? There's a bar over the door in case you haven't noticed."

"Wait until we're sure they're gone Chloe," Giselle said.

"Wait for what?" Hercule demanded. "You're going to wave a magic wand or something?"

"Not quite," Chloe chuckled and sat back down to consume her share of the food.

"You might want to save some of it," Hercule said. "That bastard Tim said we would be here a while."

"By tonight, we will be back in town," Giselle said. "I think enough time has passed, if you want to try now."

Chloe slipped her knife out of her boot again and went to the door. The space was just barely wide enough for the blade to

slip between the door and the door jamb. Gently she pried upwards until she heard the bar slip out of the slots. She pushed and the door swung wide.

The shed that had been their jail was at the end of a dirt road. A timeworn Wharf jutted out into the river. An equally ancient rowboat was tied off at the end of the pier.

It was quiet. The occasional call of a marsh bird sounded over the lap of water against the shore.

"River or road?" Chloe asked Giselle.

"All the rivers and streams around here flow toward Junction City. I say we take the boat."

"What if they took us downriver instead of up?" Hercule objected.

Giselle looked up at the sky. "We're east of the delta," she said. "Besides the stream over there isn't big enough to be Black River. We have to be up one of the tributaries to it."

Hercule hesitated. "I want to see what is at the end of this road before we take off in a rowboat."

Chloe shrugged. "Go ahead. We're going to check out the boat."

She and Giselle watched him take off down the road with a long loping stride.

"He looks like Caleb's twin," Giselle remarked. "Cousin did you say?"

"Yes. Apparently, Caleb didn't know he was in town until he asked Sheriff Melody how to contact one of the local crime bosses."

"Not a successful one, if his own men betrayed him," Giselle remarked.

"I suppose so," Chloe said absently. She was kneeling on the pier looking into the boat. "It's got oars at least," she told Giselle, "and I don't see any water in the bottom, so I think it will hold us without sinking."

"All three of us?" Hercule had returned.

"It should. What did you find at the end of the road?"

"They've set themselves up in a cabin close to where this drive intersects with a main road. My guess is it leads into Junction City."

"They rode out here. Where did they put their tricorns?" Chloe asked.

"There's a lean-to out back. If we steal the animals, we can ride back into town instead of floating down the river. I don't like boats."

"There is only two of them. We need three mounts," Chloe pointed out.

"You two are pretty light. You could ride double," he offered.

"What do you think?" Giselle asked Chloe.

"If they found our trail, I think Caleb and Henry will be coming by the road," she said.

"Okay, let's go steal some tricorns," Giselle said.

Hercule wasn't a woodsman. He kept stepping on things that crackled and made noise. In exasperation, Chloe finally told him to walk on the dirt path and meet them by the main road.

Although in better shape than the one in which Chloe and Giselle had been kept, this dwelling was rundown as well. The window on the side near the road had broken glass and the one on the side near the trees was covered with an animal skin.

The tricorns were both standing hipshot in the lean-to munching on a couple of flakes of straggly hay. The saddles had been dumped in the dirt under the edge of the lean-to.

Chloe turned each of the saddles over and brushed the dirt off the under padding as best as she could and shook out the blankets.

She slipped into the shed and slid a bridle over the nearest tricorn's head. He seemed calm enough, so she laid a blanket over his back, swung the saddle after it and then cinched up. She left him still eating and did the same with the other animal.

"The biggest danger is those two hoodlums might hear us walking by with the animals," Giselle whispered.

"Keep to the edge of the road," Chloe said. "The sand looks softer there."

It took a nerve wracking ten minutes to sneak by the cabin. Hercule met them in the road about a quarter mile from it.

Chloe handed him the reins of one of the tricorns and mounted the other. She took her foot out of the stirrup and held out her hand for Giselle to climb on behind her.

After about an hour's riding, they could just see the edge of Junction City when they met Caleb and Henry who were following Caleb's two remaining dogs who were nose down on their trail.

Henry jumped down and rushed over to help Giselle slide down from Chloe's tricorn, followed by Caleb who put his arms around Chloe and buried his face in her lap.

"Are you hurt?" he asked, his voice muffled.

She reached out and touched his hair. "I'm okay."

Caleb gave a shudder and pulled her off the tricorn. She slid down into his arms, meeting his mouth with her own.

Henry coughed. "No wish to interrupt," he said, but I need to get Giselle back to

town. I don't like the way her head is bleeding.

Caleb reluctantly lifted his head. "I haven't been so scared since I learned Julie was missing," he said.

Examining the lump on Giselle's head, Henry demanded. "Who hit you?"

Giselle leaned against his sturdy frame, grateful for the support. "It happened when they grabbed us," she said. "Athena charged and the man holding me hit me with the butt of his pistol. I'm sorry Caleb, but I think he shot her."

"He did," Caleb said. "The bullet grazed her skull. She's alive, but I took her home when we realized you'd been taken. He looked over at Chloe. "Are sure you aren't hurt?"

She shook her head. "They used chloroform on me." She gestured, "Look who joined us in our captivity."

"I saw," Caleb said. He turned to his cousin. "It looks as if your bodyguards fell down on the job. What happened."

"My bodyguards," Hercule said grimly, "are going to rue the day they did this."

"It was the two men we saw the night we met him," Chloe said.

"You'll excuse me, Cousin, but I need to get back into town and round up the rest of my men," Hercule said.

"Be careful; your cover could be

blown," Caleb warned.

Hercule nodded acknowledgement of the warning and nudged his tricorn with his heels and the animal obediently set off at a trot down the road. Caleb watched him go.

"What did you learn from Mrs. Fisher?" he asked.

"Nothing new. Giselle thinks it was a trap. They took us in her driveway."

Henry had helped Giselle onto one of the spare tricorns. "Giselle needs to see a doctor about that lump on her head," he said.

Caleb nodded. "Leave us the extra tricorn and take her back into town. Chloe can show me where these two kidnappers have taken roost. Do you know who they are waiting for?" he asked Chloe as they remounted and headed back toward the cabin.

"Tim and Les didn't talk to us. Both Giselle and I were out cold. From the stuff they said while they didn't know we'd woke up, I'm pretty sure they didn't know his identity. I'm betting they tried to take Hercule out of the game because he was close to finding out who the new player is," she said.

She ought to be thinking about the case, but her mind kept tracking back to the kiss they had exchanged when Caleb

found them.

"How come you are so good in the woods and your cousin is so awful?" she asked presently. "When we took the tricorns from the cabin corral, he made so much noise I had to make him go walk on the road."

"He's a city boy," Caleb replied softly.

"The two of you certainly took different roads after you left Copper City. Why did you warn him about his cover being blown? He *is* a crime boss, isn't he?"

"Not so different as you think; Yes, he is a crime boss, but Hercule is under cover investigating a crime syndicate we think is attempting to gain control of the City States by taking over the criminal elements in each City state. They are well protected. Posing as one of them was the only way our boss in the Enforcers could think of to find out who is actually running things."

"Why didn't you tell me before we went to meet him?"

He eyed her warily. "It didn't seem like a good time. Besides, I didn't know how good an actress you were. I couldn't chance his men suspecting anything."

"It looks as if they did anyway."

"Yeah, it does, doesn't it? I wonder where he slipped up?"

## WAY HAY & UP SHE RISES

THEY TIED the Tricorns off the road behind some large skinwood trees where they wouldn't easily be seen. Chloe led Caleb to a spot where they could watch the cabin and they sat down against the bole of a large stump.

There was an intimacy about lying here in the woods, Chloe thought. She looked up and met Caleb's eyes and realized he felt it too. He was lying down, leaning on one elbow. With his free hand he reached out and touched the dusky curls escaping from their net, liking the silky feel of her hair.

Chloe reached up and caught his hand, turning it over to she could see the tough-skinned palm.

"When did you realize we were missing?" Chloe asked him.

He turned his hand over, so they were clasping each other's hand. The gentle strength in his grip send a prickle of desire through her.

"I had an uneasy feeling all day," he admitted. When I escorted Francis back to the house, Henry told me the two of you hadn't returned from seeing Susan Fisher. He was worried.

When we checked out Fisher's house, we found Athena just waking up. Mrs. Fisher

wouldn't let us in, and she claimed she hadn't seen or heard anything. I can't remember when I've been more terrified."

"You? Terrified?" she said. "I find that hard to believe."

"Believe it," his hand tightened on hers. "I don't know how it happened. I haven't cared much about anyone since my sister Julie was killed. When I met you, it was as if I recognized you." He gave her a quick sidelong glance. "I know it's probably too soon, but I need to know if you feel the same way."

Chloe made a face. "It happened to me as well the first night in Adam's store," she said. "Giselle knew when I got home that night."

"What did she know?"

"Don't be coy," she said. "My mother told me love could happen that way, but I never thought it would happen for me. I recognized you as the man I wanted to spend the rest of my life with."

When he pulled her into his arms, she went, answering his passion with her own, and for a few minutes the world slipped away. It was the wrong time, and the wrong place.

"We can't do this here," Chloe gasped.

Reluctantly he lifted his head. "I know. We must both be crazy."

He sat up to pull himself together,

rebuttoning his shirt and tucking it back into his pants.

"Your blouse buttons are crooked," he told her.

They looked up when they heard the distinctive clip, clop of a tricorn's feet coming down the road.

Chloe glanced down at herself. "It could be Hercule coming back," she suggested, redoing her buttons.

"Maybe, but even if he is my cousin I rather he didn't see you with your clothes undone. In any case, I don't think he's had time to get back to town gather up his men and start back. I'm betting it's the man who ordered the kidnapping come to give them their payoff," he said.

A smart buggy turnout with a showy black tricorn between the shafts passed their position and trotted up to the cabin. A slim, stylishly dressed young man in a grey suit got down and went to the door. He knocked and was admitted.

Caleb stared. "I'll be damned! It's Montrose, Fisher's office clerk," he said softly.

A few minutes later the three men came out the front door and headed down the lane to the now empty cabin where Chloe and the others had been kept prisoner.

"What do you suppose is going to happen when they find we escaped?" Chloe

wondered.

"Well, I'm pretty sure they won't get paid," Caleb said dryly. "Let's get closer. Maybe we can hear what they say."

He and Chloe walked over to the side of the house nearest the trees and waited. When the three men returned, it was obvious they were in the throes of an argument.

"I tell you they have to be around here somewhere!" Tim's voice was loud.

"I don't care. The deal was for you to deliver the women and Jones. No delivery, no money."

"Maybe we ought to just take it off you anyway," Les, the shorter of Hercule's bodyguards said.

There was the sound of a scuffle, and then silence. Peering around the edge of the porch, Caleb saw only two men still standing. Surprisingly, one of the two was Fisher's clerk Montrose. He wiped his knife with a pristine white handkerchief.

"You killed him," Tim sounded stunned.

Montrose backed away and stepped into the buggy. "The boss won't be happy," he told Tim. "If you know what's good for you, you'll get your ass out of here."

He drove off, leaving Tim staring down at his buddy.

Caleb waited until the buggy had disappeared into the distance before

stepping out from the porch.

"Raise your hands," he said.

Tim did as he was told, slowly turning around to face them. "So that's how you escaped," he said, nodding a Caleb.

"No I can't take the credit; it happened before we arrived," Caleb told him.

"Chloe, get his weapons. Stand perfectly still while she works, Tim. I promise you she's just as deadly as Montrose."

"Montrose. Is that his name?"

"Yes," Caleb watched critically as Chloe removed two guns and a knife from Tim's person, doing a much better job of looking for hidden weapons than he had when he had searched her.

"Hold out your hands," she instructed. When he did, She tied his wrists together with a thin rope.

"Go and get the tricorns," Caleb told Chloe.

When she was out of hearing, he studied Tim thoughtfully. The flat assessing stare made Tim uneasy and he shifted from foot to foot. Finally he blurted out, "What are you going to do with me?"

"Well, I think Sheriff Melody will have plenty to charge you with. Let's see; there is Kidnapping, and assault on a woman resulting in a concussion and might

have killed her. And oh yes, you shot my dog."

"I didn't shoot the dog!" Tim's voice squeaked. "I didn't hit the old woman either! Les did it!"

Chloe had ridden up on Trisket, leading Caleb's big stallion and the gelding she had stolen from the lean-to behind the cabin.

"Do you want to search the cabin before we leave?" she asked.

"Might as well," Caleb agreed. He gestured with his pistol for Tim to proceed them into the cabin.

The rooms had once been neatly kept. Tim and Les hadn't had much time to make a mess. Chloe banked the fire in the stove, covering the bluestones with a layer of soda powder to put out the heat. She threw the small supply of perishable food the men had brought with them out the back door where a flock of wild hens soon disposed of it.

The remainder of the house turned up nothing, but a deed made out to someone named Hortense Dubarry.

"Leave it in the drawer where you found it," Caleb ordered. "We can do a search for relatives in the town archives."

Chloe packed the remaining dried meat and cheese hunks into a canvas sack and tied it to the back of Trisket's saddle.

She and Caleb took turns keeping an eye on Tim while the other one mounted.

"Ride in front of us," Caleb instructed. "Remember I'm a good shot and so is Chloe."

"You just going to leave him there?" Tim pointed to the hapless Les's body.

"The Sheriff will want to see it the way it happened," Caleb replied. "I don't want to disturb his crime scene."

"But what if the animals get him?" Tim protested.

"Guess that's life," Caleb replied. "Get moving; we've got an hours ride ahead of us."

By the time Henry and Giselle had arrived back at her house, Giselle was exhausted. Only her iron will had kept her in the saddle for the journey. She was too tired to get off the tricorn on her own and sat slumped in the saddle. Henry dismounted and moved quickly to help her. He slid an arm around her back and lifted her off the saddle, catching and supporting her legs with his other arm.

When he mounted the steps with his burden, an anxious Mrs. Syms threw open the door.

"What happened to her?" she cried. "Where's Miss Chloe?"

Before Henry could answer, a chorus of similar questions erupted from Francis,

Hetty and Sydney. Kimi came out from under the chair and jumped up at him, worriedly trying to see Giselle.

Giselle lifted her head from Henry's shoulder. "I'm alright. I'm just tired. I just need some sleep."

"She took a knock on the head. Send Tom for the doctor and the sheriff," Henry ordered. "And one of you come up to her room to help me get her into bed."

"What happened to Chloe?" Francis demanded.

"She stayed with Caleb. She was okay when I saw her. Will someone catch this blasted critter before I trip over her?" he added irascibly.

Hetty caught Kimi in mid bound, holding her up out of the way despite her frantic efforts to get to Giselle. The three girls followed Henry and his burden up the stairs. When she saw the door to the room she was sharing with Lila close as they mounted the stairs, Francis grimaced. Taking the coward's way out as usual, she thought.

Henry set a tired Giselle gently on the edge of the bed and knelt to pull off her boots. She stretched out a hand and touched his hair tenderly.

"You always come to my rescue," she said ruefully.

He turned his face into her hand. "You

need to be more careful; you could have been killed this time."

"I don't think he was supposed to hit me, he had a chloroform rag in his hand. He dropped it and drew the gun when Athena charged him. Did I hear you say she was alive?"

Henry stood up and stepped back out of Francis's way. "Yes, the bullet just creased her skull. Lucky she has a hard head. Almost as hard as yours."

Giselle gave a weak chuckle and reached out to pat Kimi when Hetty set her on the bed. The younger girl went to the dresser and pulled out a soft nightgown.

"Lizette and I can manage this if you will step out into the hall," Francis told Henry over her shoulder as she unbuttoned Giselle's blouse.

"You're lucky you only got hit in the head," Lizette scolded as she tenderly turned down the bed.

Henry grinned a little as he stepped out of the room. He wanted no part of what was about to happen: Lizette loved Giselle like a sister, and he was confident she would take excellent care of her, but Giselle was in for a rare scolding for having worried her. He went down to put the tricorns in the stable.

Tom had mounted Lizette's tricorn and he rode out of the stable just as Henry

entered leading the two tired animals. He made quick work of unsaddling them and rubbing them down and turned them into stalls, adding a flake of hay to each manger. Remembering he had promised Caleb he would check on Athena, he looked over the rim of the stall they had made into a temporary kennel. She lifted her head and wagged her tail when she saw him.

He returned to the house just as Doctor Sanderson arrived. "Come on in Doctor. Lizette and Francis should have Giselle made decent by now."

"What happened to her?" Sanderson asked. "The boy didn't know; just that you carried her into the house."

"She and Miss Chloe were kidnapped yesterday. Giselle took a clout to the skull."

When Caleb and Chloe arrived at the sheriff's office with their prisoner, Melody was waiting for them, having already taken a statement from an irate Henry and a sleepy Giselle whom Doctor Sanderson had ordered to stay in bed for a few days.

"I see you found your partner," he said. "Is this the kidnapper?"

When Chloe nodded, he asked, "Miss DeMille are you pressing charges against this man?"

"Yes," she replied. "I will make a

statement, but I would like to check on Giselle's condition first."

"I've already been to the house to get her statement," Melody said. "Henry took her home and put her to bed. The doc says she will be fine with some rest."

Despite having gotten most of the same information from Giselle, it was several hours later when Caleb and Chloe were free to go to the house, where they were greeted by an anxious Mrs. Syms and an excited Kimi.

"Are you alright, Miss Chloe?" Mrs. Syms asked.

"I'm fine," Chloe assured her, dodging Kimi's exuberant tongue. "We could use something to eat though. How is Giselle?"

"Asleep," Mrs. Syms said. "Lizette is sitting with her. As for food, I have stew warming on the stove. I'll have it on the table in a few minutes. Joe," she called to her son. "Give the Tricorns a bait of feed and give those dogs some of the food left for Athena."

"How is she doing?" Caleb asked the boy.

"She ate okay," he replied. "I doctored her head like you said to."

"I checked on her after I put Giselle to bed. She looks fine," Henry said, joining them at the table.

As soon as everyone was seated, Mrs.

Syms ladled generous servings of a hearty chicken stew accompanied by warm cornbread muffins into bowls and passed them around.

## THICKENING SHADOWS

CALEB HAD enjoyed his breakfast the next morning. George was a real find. "So tell me," he asked the cook as he dumped hot water over a load of breakfast dishes, "why aren't you cooking for some fancy restaurant?"

"Well, I used to, but after I told off a couple of diners who wanted to tell me how to cook, I decided I didn't want to work for a bunch of ingrates who couldn't tell a poached egg from fried."

"Their loss is my gain," Caleb said. After checking on the tricorns and bringing his two remaining dogs into the office, he walked into the reception area. It was empty. He frowned when he realized Jim Billing was late again.

Caleb sat down at the desk and checked the contents of the reports he had assigned Billing to type up. None of them had been done. From the looks of things, Billing hadn't managed to get the typewriter ribbon threaded. He also found a half empty bottle of whiskey in a bottom drawer. Well it was a shame, but he had gotten lucky with two of the workers Binns had recommended. He was going to need to find a replacement for Billing.

When Jim Billing finally arrived, he stopped, teetering on the threshold when

he saw Caleb sitting at the desk.

"You're late," Caleb said. "The office opened an hour ago."

Billing blinked owlishly at him. "S-sorry," he said. "I overslept."

Caleb took the half-empty whiskey bottle out of the drawer and set it on the desk. "I was looking for the typewriter ribbon when I found this. Is it yours?"

"I just need a little pick me up occasionally, that's all."

Caleb laid three silver chips on the desk. "I'm sorry, but I can't allow drinking on the job. Here's your severance pay."

Billing glared at him. "Think you're pretty tough, do you?"

Caleb just looked at him. Billings grabbed the chips off the desk, wheeled around, almost falling as he did so, and stumbled back out the door, almost running into Hercule who was coming into the building.

Caleb looked up at his cousin.

"You're taking a chance coming here in person."

Hercule laughed. "My cover's blown. Somebody you spoke to recognized the family resemblance and put two and two together. It's all over the criminal underworld this morning I'm an Enforcer. So I came here to see if you had any useful

ideas."

"Did you find out anything at all about the new syndicate?"

Hercule shook his head. "Nothing new, just the rumor someone is trying to organize the criminal element to take over the City States. If there is an organized plan, it's still deep under cover. I could never get an invite to any meetings, and I'm pretty sure I won't now."

"Well, we'll just have to figure something else out," Caleb said. "Your showing up just now is fortuitous for me; I just had to fire my receptionist for being drunk on the job. I had originally planned to continue to help Melody search for Larry Dominique, but I need someone to hold down the fort here until I can hire a new man."

"Sure, why not?" Hercule said. "Do I get lunch?"

"Yes. You're in for a treat. George is a fabulous cook."

"Excellent. How did the ladies survive our adventure?"

"Giselle is back to normal after the knock she took on her head. Chloe wasn't hurt; just chloroformed to put her out. She told me she would be helping Francis enroll her sisters in the local school today. At the dance, Francis said she would be looking for work. I thought I

would ask her if she would consider working here as a receptionist."

"Isn't she the daughter of the man who killed his wife and Judson? Having her work here might be taken as a conflict of interest. Can you trust her not to hinder the plan to locate her father?"

"From what I gather, none of the girls are close to their father. He seems to have spent a lot of time away from home. Not to change the subject, but before the rumors broke your cover did you hear any chitchat about any strangers watching the night ladies or hiding out in Docktown?"

Hercule sat down on the corner of the desk while he considered the question. "You might try Louella Bates. She runs a saloon down near the railroad. For the right price she might hide him."

"Thanks, I'll tell Melody."

When Caleb arrived at Chloe's house, he found Francis and Chloe attempting to get the girls ready to attend school.

"Are you still looking for work?" he asked Francis.

"Yes, do you know of something?"

"I need a receptionist for the Enforcer's office," he said. "The man I hired came to work drunk and I fired him. My cousin will be holding down the fort for a few days, but he's primarily an investigator."

"When do you want me to start?"

"As soon as you get your sisters settled. How does the day after tomorrow sound? The office opens at nine."

"I'll be there," Francis assured him. "Girls, go and wash up. The rickshaw we ordered will be here any minute."

"I thought we were hiding the fact your cousin was undercover," Chloe remarked.

"His cover got blown when I came to town," Caleb explained. "It's unfortunate the family resemblance is so strong; someone apparently realized we are related and now everyone suspects he is an Enforcer."

"Why was he posing as a crime boss?"

"He was here to try and infiltrate a crime syndicate spreading over the City States."

"Did you know he was here?" Francis asked.

Caleb smiled ruefully. "Not until Chloe and I walked into the warehouse the other night. Sometimes the Enforcer Bureau doesn't tell the right hand what the left is doing."

"So what is he going to do next?" Chloe asked.

"I'm going to try and get him reassigned to this office permanently. Hercule thinks if the Bureau will send another agent down here (not a Jones), we

might still be able to get evidence against Councilman Fisher."

"Is he the one you suspect of being the head of the new syndicate?" Giselle asked.

"Yes, but suspicion isn't proof. We need facts before we can move on him. He and his wife can't even be held accountable because you were kidnapped out of their driveway. In the meantime, Hercule gave me a name to ask where your father might be hiding," Caleb told Francis, who made a quick movement of protest when she saw her sister's shocked faces in the doorway. "It's for his protection as well. Judson had friends who might want revenge for his death," he added to reassure the younger girls. Sydney looked relieved, but Hetty, who was a lot like Francis in temperament still frowned.

Francis nodded soberly, "I understand."

When Caleb left the house, he met Melody and Hercule in Melody's office.

"What's he doing here?" Melody demanded, staring at Hercule.

"Sheriff Melody, meet Enforcer Hercule Jones. Hercule has been undercover trying to get a lead on a new crime syndicate the Bureau thinks is forming."

"Why wasn't I told about this?" Melody challenged.

"I didn't tell you because I didn't

know about it," Caleb said.

Hercule lifted a hand. "In cases like this where a deep cover is required, we don't tell anyone; especially since we didn't know who all the players were before I arrived. For all I knew, you or one of your men could have been in on it or at least passing on information."

Melody scowled, but although he was lawman enough to see the justice of this, he was still left with a feeling of ill-usage.

"Is he coming with us?"

"You'll need me when you question Louella," Hercule said. "We were friends of a sort."

"I can just imagine," Melody said sourly.

Louella Bates, who owned the Broken Bit Saloon, was a tall, robustly build woman. Her red hair, which she scorned to dye, had a touch of grey. A scar across one cheek added to her formidable appearance.

It was before noon when Caleb and the other two lawmen arrived. Louella was just wiping down the pale skinwood bar and two of her workers were clearing up debris from last night's customers. Both men had shirt sleeves rolled up revealing heavily muscled forearms. Leather covered wooden clubs dangled from each man's belt.

Louella looked up as the trio entered.

Her gaze settled accusingly on Hercule. "You've got a lot of nerve coming in here, Jones," she said.

Hercule grinned at her. "Oh, don't tell me I fooled you about what I am; you're too smart for that."

Louella snorted. "What do you want?"

"Information," Caleb said. He took out a small bag of silver chips and set it on the bar. Louella's eyes flickered with interest, but she didn't reach for it.

"I don't stoolie," she said. "If I started telling the law all I know my customers wouldn't trust me."

"I doubt this man is one of your regulars," Hercule said. "His name is Larry Dominique and we think he killed his wife. Cut her up with a knife. He killed Levi Judson too."

Her eyes narrowed. "Levi had a couple of buddies who were in here looking for him last night. What's this Dominique look like?"

"He's around forty, with pale skin, grey eyes and thin blond hair. He usually wears a suit and tie."

She frowned, absently continuing to wipe down the bar. "Hey Jeb," she called, "didn't you say a stranger had rented one of Sara's cribs?"

"Yeah," he replied. "Said he gave her the creeps, but his money was good."

"Where do we find this Sara?" Melody spoke for the first time.

"Down two blocks and around the corner," the other man volunteered.

"Thank you, Louella. I'll remember this," Hercule said.

"Better not," she retorted. "It's bad for my image to be seen with the likes of you."

Hercule laughed, picking up her hand, oily rag and all and kissed it, before turning to follow his cousin and Melody out through the batwing doors. Louella swiped the bag of coins off the bar and stuck into her apron pocket.

While the three lawmen were speaking to Sara, Chloe and Francis had finally gotten the girls settled in the rickshaw and started for the school.

"We're going to be late," Francis prophesized. "I hope it doesn't mean it's a bad omen."

She and Chloe had chosen to ride behind the rickshaw. "It will be fine," Chloe said. The rickshaw driver was traveling at a smooth ground eating trot, forcing the tricorns to do the same.

River Junction Elementary School was located on the outskirts of the city next to the Red Rock District, where the most affluent residents of Junction City had homes. It was a three-story building with a tree shaded yard for the children to play in. While some parents, such as Cora Dominique preferred to home school their children, most of the parents in the area banded together to hire teachers and rent a large house whose rooms served as classrooms. It had the advantage of a kitchen whose workforce provided lunch for staff and students. The three teachers were to instruct the younger children in basic reading, writing, and mathematics. Older children were also taught the history of St. Antoni and an overview of what had led to the settlement of the planet. The children were provided an explanation of the Portal Settlement Act and what its effect on the citizens of St. Antoni would be if Earth discovered the illegal colony.

When Francis and Chloe arrived with the girls, they were shown into the administrator's office. The woman was about forty, with unnaturally dark hair worn in a tight braid around the crown of her head. She was about Chloe's height and dressed in a dark grey shirt tucked into grey pants. She wore a pair of serviceable shoes.

"Good morning," she said, nodding at the chairs in front of her desk. "Please take a seat. I'm Mrs. Edmonton, the administrator for River Junction

Elementary School. What can I do for you today?"

"I'd like to enroll my sisters in your school," Francis said. She pointed at two chairs along the wall. Hetty and Sydney sat down gingerly.

"Do you have custody? Where are your parents?" Mrs. Edmonton asked.

"My mother is dead, and my father is missing," Francis replied.

"My secretary said your name was Dominique. At River Junction we pride ourselves in only accepting children with a good background. I am acquainted with almost everyone in this parish who has school age children and I don't recognize your name. Do you have any references?"

Chloe pulled a sheaf of letters out of her purse. "I believe you will find these references satisfactory."

Mrs. Edmonton opened the letters and read through them meticulously. "I see here you have a reference from Amy Wong, the head of the Women's Circle, Giselle St. Vyr and also one from Councilman Fisher's wife."

Francis mouth dropped open, but she quickly shut it when Chloe tapped her ankle with her foot. She hadn't known about the letters of reference. She waited without answering.

After a few minutes, Mrs. Edmonton

spoke, "I believe these will be sufficient. How much schooling have they had?" she studied the two girls who fidgeted under her assessing gaze.

"My mother home schooled them," Francis replied. "They have had a good grounding in reading and arithmetic and some schooling in history."

Mrs. Edmonton frowned. "We will have to test them to see what levels they have progressed to. It's a necessary procedure with all incoming homeschooled students."

"She rang′ a small bell on her desk, and her secretary, a thin young woman with a nervous tic beside her mouth entered the room. "Linda, this is Hetty and Sydney Dominique. They are new students. They've been home schooled, so please arrange testing for them so we can place them in the proper classes."

"Yes, Mrs. Edmonton. Girls, if you will follow me?"

Hetty and Sydney rose and followed her out of the room.

"Now, school fees are due monthly. They include lunch prepared here at the school and supplies and books. The monthly payments—"

She stopped when Chloe rose and dropped a small bag of coins and gems on the desk.

"I believe you will find the contents of this bag sufficient to cover any costs.

Please give me a receipt."

"Of course." Mrs. Edmonton rang the bell again and an older woman entered. She had a pair of pince-nez spectacles perched on her nose. "Ladies this is Mrs. Carvers. She is our accountant. This is for school fees for two students. The ladies require a receipt."

"Of course. If you will come with me, we'll get that done."

"Thank you for your time, Mrs. Edmonton," Chloe said as she and Francis followed the other woman out of the office.

Outside the school, Francis made an appointment for the rickshaw driver to collect the two girls and bring them home after school ended for the day.

"Let's head on over to the office so you can get acquainted with what Caleb wants you to do," suggested Chloe.

"Alright," Francis said, going on to ask the question she had been dying to ask since Chloe produced the reference letters. "How did Giselle get Mrs. Fisher to give us a reference? Isn't her husband the man who arranged to kidnap you?"

Chloe chuckled. "Never underestimate Giselle. I saw the letter she sent requesting the reference. It started out with 'I'm sure you will be glad to know I have recovered from my ordeal when I was kidnapped in your driveway.'"

"So she threatened her?"

Chloe laughed. "Yes, but you'll note the threat was never overtly stated. When you spend more time around her, you'll find out Giselle is a master at getting people to do what she wants them to."

She and Francis were just dismounting in front of the office when Deputy Raymond Cortez hurried across the street to meet them.

"Hello," he said. "I don't know if you remember me—"

"Of course," Chloe answered. "Francis you remember Deputy Cortez. He was introduced to you at the dance."

"Yes, you danced with my sister Lila. How are you Deputy?" Francis asked.

"I wanted to tell you how sorry I am about what happened to your parents," he said.

"Thank you," Francis said. She turned to follow Chloe into the office but stopped when he spoke again.

"I was wondering if—"

Francis turned to face him. Standing on the boardwalk in front of the office she was almost at eye level with him. "If what, Deputy?"

"How is Miss Lila?" he asked.

"It was a great shock to a girl with

her delicate temperament," Francis let the words fall with practiced ease. "I'll tell her you asked about her."

"I'd like to tell her myself," he said. "If she's feeling up to callers."

"My sister doesn't remember what happened," Francis said bluntly. "The doctor called it hysterical amnesia. If you're going to ask her questions about it, I'm afraid the answer is no."

To her surprise the young man flushed. "No!" he exclaimed. "I won't pester her with questions about it. I just wanted to see her again."

A tall man had come out of the office. Seeing him out of the corner of her eye, Francis thought it was Caleb and his presence gave her courage. "Are you asking me if you can court my sister Deputy?"

"Yes," he admitted. "I won't say or do anything to upset her, I promise."

"You may come for tea next Saturday," she said. "no earlier than three in the afternoon and no later than four."

When she turned around, she was startled to realize the man who had come out of the office wasn't Caleb. This man resembled him, but he was better looking. There was a decided twinkle in his eye, and he had dimples when he smiled.

"Hello," she said. "Who are you?"

Hercule laughed and swept her a bow.

"Hercule Jones at your service. You must be Francis."

"Are you Caleb's brother?" she asked, passing through the door he was holding open for her.

"Cousin actually, but our mothers were identical twins." he said, letting the door swing closed in the Deputy's face.

## A LIGHT IN THE DARKNESS

RAYMOND CORTEZ showed up for tea exactly on time. He had brought Lila a vase of roses. Watching her sister respond to the young man's attention gave Francis a sharp stab of relief. She hoped being courted would do much to bring Lila back to her normal self.

Caleb and Hercule also showed up for the repast. Both men appeared to be quite content to join in the family collation and Hercule allowed himself to be inveigled into helping with a jigsaw puzzle the girls had started.

Chloe glanced into the Library where the puzzle had been laid out on a long table. "Your cousin seems to be enjoying this," she told Caleb.

"He is. So am I. since the war with the Smith's tore our family apart, we haven't had an opportunity to just do family things like a puzzle with Francis's sisters. It makes a nice change."

"I hope you and your cousin will consider us as family," Giselle said with a smile.

"I understand why you split up leaving Copper city, but why didn't your family make plans to meet somewhere after they were safe?" Francis asked.

Caleb smiled wryly. "Because some of

the family is still in danger. Kicking us out of Copper City wasn't the Smith's only goal in the war. They also wanted control of the Jones Hoard." At her puzzled look, he went on, "over the years we controlled Copper City, the family amassed a considerable amount of money and important documents."

"Why didn't you take it with you?"

"There wasn't time to go and get it from where it was hidden. The Smiths were already watching where we went. They are still attempting to locate a couple of our older aunts who they think might know the location."

"You mean it's still in Copper City? What if someone stumbles on it?"

"Well, we didn't abandon it; we left a family member guarding it. According to Ezekiel, no one has come near it."

"Who is Ezekiel?" Chloe asked.

"Ezekiel is our great uncle. He was chosen to guard the Hoard for two reasons; he's always been something of a hermit, and he doesn't look like the rest of us. He took after his mother's side of the family."

Later, Chloe examined Kimi's leg to see how well it was healing. "Do you think she's ready for the cast to come off?" she asked Giselle.

Giselle took the fox's leg between her

fingers and pressed firmly. "She's not showing any discomfort, so I think it's healed. We just need to make sure she doesn't reinjure it for a few weeks."

After removing the cast, Chloe set the fox down on the floor and cleaned up the debris.

She and Giselle were alone in the library. Henry and the girls had already gone up to bed.

"Something is bothering you, my dear. Care to tell me about it?"

Chloe hesitated. "I think Caleb is becoming interested in me personally, and I like it."

"That's a good thing. Most women need a satisfying personal relationship to be content with life. And Caleb already knows about your past and what you do. How do you feel about him?"

"I think I'm in love with him."

"So what is the problem?"

Chloe sighed. "You said he is aware of my past, but he hasn't *seen* it in action. He's a straightforward person. He's also overprotective. I know I'm going to find it stifling after a while."

Giselle looked at her thoughtfully. "You're doubting his ability to make a commitment, aren't you?"

"It isn't just him, I'm not sure I can

maintain a good bond with him if he keeps attempting to put me in a glass case."

"Chloe, I'm an old woman and if there is one thing I've learned in life, the risks you didn't take are the ones you regret the most."

She kissed the girl on the temple and went upstairs to her room. She found Henry, sitting in a chair near the bed reading. He set the book aside and went to help her undress.

"I told Lizette she could go to bed," he said, starting to unhook her dress.

"If you're going to be with me every night, you might just as well move your things in here. It's not as if our relationship is a secret anymore," she said.

"I don't think it ever was much of a secret anyway," he replied.

The next day being Sunday, the family attended services at a local church. To Chloe's surprise, both Caleb and Hercule turned up to sit with them. After the service, the church ladies held a social gathering. Everyone had brought food to share, and when the meal was over, the children played games, several of the older ladies organized a quilting bee, and an informal square dance started.

"I haven't met half of these people," Lila whispered to Francis. "Would mother approve of them?"

"It doesn't matter what mother would have thought," Francis told her. "These are our neighbors and I hope some of them will be our friends. I expect you to be polite and friendly."

Lila flinched at Francis' sharp tone; however, she was a biddable girl who was used to having a stronger personality tell her what to do. When a young man, the son of a storekeeper came up and asked her to join in the dancing, she agreed, and was soon laughing and having a good time with a group of young people.

"Wow!" Hercule said. He had been standing behind Francis and overheard her order to Lila. "You're a bossy thing, aren't you?"

Francis flushed in embarrassment. "My relationship with my sister is none of your business."

He held up both hands. "Don't shoot, It was just an observation. From what I saw, she needs a guiding hand. I guess you're it."

"I'm sorry," Francis said. "I suppose I am bossy. I got in the habit of making decisions for the four of us because Mother was only interested in finding us good marriages. She was kind of oblivious to anything not directly impacting getting us married."

He looked at her curiously. "Back home one of our Aunts usually handled making marriage deals for the family. Is that what you want for yourself and your sisters? To get married?"

"For Lila certainly; I think it will be the only way she will be happy. I plan on encouraging Hetty and Sydney to give their other interests free rein."

"And for yourself?"

She smiled wryly. "Someone has to run the show. I think I've been nominated for the post."

"For what it's worth, I think you are doing a fine job with Hetty and Sydney."

"Thank you," she said in surprise.

He held out a hand. "That dance looks like fun. Care to join me?"

"You'll be sorry; although I love to dance, I'm told I'm not I'm not the best dancer in the world."

Hercule laughed. "I'll chance it."

Caleb and Chloe had walked away from the group towards the river. It made a soft gurgling sound blending with the laughter and the music from the dance.

When Caleb had suggested they take a stroll, Chloe had welcomed the suggestion. She wanted to talk about Larry Dominique and with Francis and her sisters in the house, privacy for discussions such as the one she intended to have were few and far between.

Pursuant of this, she asked, "Do you think Larry Dominque killed his wife?"

Caleb looked down at the top of her flowered hat with a grimace. He had had other ideas for this interlude; ideas which hadn't included a discussion of murderers.

"We don't know. We don't have any real evidence against him. It's all circumstantial; without Lila's testimony we can't even prove he killed his wife. Right now, all Melody wants to do is talk to him."

"You're hoping he will give something away during interrogation, aren't you?"

"Yes," Caleb admitted.

"What about the prostitute murders? Do you have any suspects?"

He frowned. "The murders are similar to ones which took place in Azure City and Bitterstown over the last few years. Before I came here, I was investigating them."

"Isn't it unusual for a serial killer to change his hunting grounds so drastically?"

"It is. It wasn't just prostitutes being killed though. I'm convinced about half of the murders were paid killings."

A sharp stab of fear flicked Chloe. She knew at least one of the deaths in Azure City, that of Ira Johnson, had been paid for, because she had done it. She needed to learn what Caleb knew about Johnson's case.

"Could I look through your notes? Maybe I'll see something you didn't."

"Fresh eyes are always a help," Caleb agreed. "Come by the office tomorrow and I'll let you read through them."

A layer of fine sand edged this section of the riverbank, creating a nice stretch of beach where couples and families could enjoy a picnic. Just now it was deserted; anyone enjoying the beach today had been drawn up to the church yard by the music.

Caleb slipped an arm around Chloe's waist. "I didn't intend for us to spend our time discussing murder," he said.

She looked up at him. "What did you intend doing?"

"This." He lowered his head and she lifted her mouth to meet his. It was a slow, deep kiss. When he pulled her gently down on the sand, she went willingly.

While Chloe and Francis were getting better acquainted with the Jones men, Gerald Fisher was questioning his aid about them.

Gerald Fisher eyed Gavin Montrose across his desk. "You're sure about it?"

he asked.

Montrose nodded. "Yes, Hercule Jones is staying at the Enforcer office with his cousin.

One thing about Montrose, Fisher reflected, he was an efficient devil. He had hired him originally because he needed a liaison between himself and his criminal enterprises. Despite his effeminate, dandified appearance, the man was a ruthless killer. It soon became obvious Montrose was also ambitious, and he had decided to hitch his star to Fisher. If the ambition didn't get out of hand, it didn't bother Fisher. He was a careful man however, and as a precaution, he had Montrose watched unobtrusively by another of his aides.

"How much did Hercule Jones find out about our organization?" he asked. "Did he know about the plan to take control of the City states?"

Montrose shrugged. "I'm not sure. If he knows anything. Whatever he discovered though, you can be sure he's already told his cousin and the woman Enforcer. I do know Caleb Jones sent off a runner to Gateway City soon after Hercule Jones got away from those two idiots we hired to kidnap him."

Gerald frowned, tapping his fingers on his desk. "It's time to get rid of all

three of them; both the Jones' men and the woman Enforcer too."

"If we kill them, Melody will investigate it and he won't give up easily."

"I want you to handle it yourself this time. We'll make it look like a rescue attempt that went wrong."

"How do you want to do it?"

"The girl Jones hired as a receptionist has two younger sisters attending the Junction City Elementary School. Grab them on the way home from school and take them out to the house in the Delta. We'll send a ransom note requiring the woman and the Jones men to come alone. Once they arrive you can take them out."

Chloe was reading through Caleb's notes on the Johnson death when word came in from a runner sent by Louella Bates. The runner was a thin, middle aged man with sharp grey eyes and a scraggly goatee.

"I'm looking for Hercule Jones," he said.

Hercule looked up from typing his report on the Syndicate investigation. He was using the typewriter on Francis's desk because the others ordered hadn't yet arrived. "What have you got Sims?" he asked.

"Lou said to tell you Dominique is in the crib he rented. She doesn't know how

long he'll be there so if you want him, you should get your ass in gear."

"Thanks," Hercule flipped him a handful of copper chips, which Sims caught with the ease of long practice.

When Hercule went into Caleb's office, the man left. Francis was setting out cups and sugar on a side table in the reception area and heard the man's message.

She took her hands off the dishware she had been setting out, and sat down hard in one of the guest chairs. She folded her hands tightly in her lap, struggling to control her breathing.

Caleb, Chloe and Hercule passed through reception area on the way to collect their tricorns.

"Did you find father?" Francis asked.

"We know where he is," Hercule said.

Francis swallowed. "What happens now?"

"That's going to be up to him," he told her gently. "Right now, Melody just wants to question him about your mother's death."

She nodded silently.

Awkwardly, he patted her shoulder. "We'll do the best we can not to hurt him," he said."

"I know," she whispered.

After they left, Francis was too restless to type the rest of the letter

she had written to her mother's family telling them about Cora's death. She got up and began the mindless task of cleaning all the dirty dishes out of the offices and taking them to the kitchen.

George looked up from prepping vegetables for lunch when she brought in a pile of dirty dishes.

"You didn't have to do that Miss Francis," he said.

"I know," she said, "but they found my father. I wanted to take my mind of what's about to happen."

George looked down at his work ruefully. "No one will be here for lunch?" he asked.

"Just me and you," she said. "And I'm not awfully hungry."

# THE GAME'S AFOOT!

MELODY AND five of his deputies met Hercule, Chloe and Caleb in Docktown just outside a weather-beaten slat house with several broken windows in the upper story. The landlord, Sara Michaels, was waiting for them.

Melody directed the men to split up and surround the house on all four sides. The house had two doors, one in the front on the tumbledown porch and one in the rear leading into the kitchen. Melody ordered two men to watch the sides of the house without doors and divided the others into teams to make entry through the doors.

"We don't know what weapons he carrying," he warned his men. "We know he has a knife; he may have a gun as well. Be careful and watch each other's backs."

"If you damage my property, I expect you to pay for it," Sara trenchantly informed Melody. She went on to enumerate the various ways law enforcement had damaged property in the area and refused to pay for repairs, declaring it wasn't going to happen to her.

When he got tired of listening to her rant, Melody said, "Old woman, if you don't shut up, I'll arrest you for harboring a fugitive."

Chloe, Caleb and Hercule were assigned

the side with a kitchen door. Melody and the other three deputies would go in the front.

When they entered the kitchen, Chloe smelled dry wood rot and dust. It was empty but a dirty plate had been left on the sideboard and several more were in the metal dishpan.

"He's not much of a housekeeper," Hercule said, wrinkling his nose.

Caleb touched his finger to the food on the plate. "This is recent," he said, wiping his hand on a dirty towel hanging from a cabinet door.

Chloe heard a noise from the pantry and made a shushing motion at them. She jerked open the door and a feral bobcat weighing nearly thirty pounds leaped out, almost knocking her down.

They heard Melody and his crew bursting in the front door and joined them in clearing the downstairs rooms. They didn't find Dominique, but one of the rooms held some grisly trophies. Arranged in specimen jars on a shelf were women's ring fingers, some of them with the rings still attached. The smell of a half open jar of formaldehyde permeated the room. One of the deputies gagged when he saw the jars.

"Never mind that," Melody said harshly. "We need to clear upstairs."

The three deputies headed for the

second story.

There was yell From the landing and shots rang out. Chloe followed Caleb as he and the deputies rushed up them. When they reached the upper hall, they found two of the deputies rolling on the floor in the corridor trying to subdue a screaming Larry Dominique. Another deputy was sitting against the wall, holding his head. Melody, and Caleb joined in the group attempting to subdue Dominique. Chloe decided she would only be in the way, so she dropped by the deputy holding his head. It was Raymond Cortez.

"Did he hit you?" she asked.

"No, I hit my head on the damn table when he jumped me," he said in disgust, indicating the shambles of what had once been a nice wooden side table. "Stunned me for a second. I shot at him on the way down, but I don't think I hit him."

"You're going to have a lump, and it will probably be sore for a while," Chloe told him, examining it.

The deputies had managed to restrain Larry Dominique, but he continued to fight the manacles they clipped on him. After one of the deputies suffered a kick in the groin from the prisoner, Melody directed for Dominique's feet be bound also. When he tried to bite the man securing him, Melody added a gag order to the

restraints.

They carried him down the stairs and dropped him into the waiting paddy wagon.

"Take him out to Rackham," Melody ordered. "Tell Dr. Kirkham he's not to be left unguarded; he's dangerous and needs a straight-jacket."

Hercule had stayed in Dominique's workroom while the rest of the team had chased the fugitive upstairs.

"Look here," he said, holding up a bound sheaf of papers. "I think it's Dominique's diary of his kills."

"Are Levi Judson and Cora Dominique in there?" Caleb asked.

"Yes, some others I think you'll find of interest as well." He gestured to the specimen jars. "Those were trophies he took from the girls he killed. See that numbered tag? There is a matching number in the diary. He lists other kills in the diary, but he didn't take trophies from them. I think we've found your hired killer Caleb."

Cortez ducked his head back in the room, "Sheriff, Doimer is out front. He took some photos of us bringing Dominique out. He wants to know if he can come inside to take photos in here."

"I'll talk to him," Melody said. He left the room.

Hercule turned to Caleb who was

scanning the diary. "We need a copy of the book. Do you suppose Melody would let us get Doimer to take photos of it for us?"

When a tired, dirty trio arrived back at the office, Francis jumped up anxiously. "Are you alright?" she asked.

"Yes, we're fine," Hercule assured her.

"And my father?"

"He's fine too. We caught him."

"He wasn't hurt, at least not more than a few bruises, but—" Caleb stopped, at a loss at what to tell her.

"There's something else, isn't there?" she asked.

Chloe put an arm around her. "Yes, there is. Come into my office."

She shut the door after them, effectively closing out the men, who exchanged relieved glances, glad to be spared the ordeal of explaining to Francis that her father had been both a hired killer and a serial murderer of prostitutes.

There was an outcry of denial from Francis, and they could hear her sobbing.

Hercule looked at his cousin. "Maybe we should—"

Caleb shook his head. "Let Chloe handle it. It will come better from her, I think. Let's get cleaned up so we can write up our reports for Rodríguez in Gateway

City."

Two days later, he heard from Rodriguez that similar crimes had been committed in several of the City States. He only had confirmation Dominque had been in Azure City and in Gateway itself on dates matching the killings in the diary."

"It isn't proof," he said when he showed the message to Chloe and Hercule, "but I think it will stand up as circumstantial evidence."

The communication also included an order assigning Hercule Jones permanently to the Enforcer Office in Junction City.

# EARLY IN THE MORNING

JEFFREY DOIMER'S photos of the house where Larry Dominique had been captured made the front page of the Junction Tribune. An excited Tom brought it inside just as they were finishing breakfast.

"Look, you made the paper!" he exclaimed, pointing out the photo of Larry Dominique as he was being put into the Sheriff's paddy wagon. There was a second shot of the shelf with the jars of women's fingers, and below it a photo of Cora Dominique in all her bloody glory. He spread it out on the breakfast table so everyone could see it.

Lila took one look at it and screamed. She followed this up by collapsing in a dead faint.

Francis said something unprintable concerning her sister, and ordered Tom to go and get some smelling salts from his mother.

"Is she going to die?" Sydney asked fearfully.

"Nonsense! It's just a faint," Giselle said.

"I think the girls ought to stay home today," Henry said. "There's a passel of reporters out front. I don't think the school has the kind of security needed to keep them off the grounds."

"Oh dear," Giselle said. "If they miss a couple of days it might put them behind on their lessons."

"I'll drop by the school and pick up their assignments," he offered.

"I suppose it will have to do," she agreed. "Are those people out back as well?"

He shook his head. "Nope, I think it'll be safe for Chloe and Francis to leave by the back gate when they go to work."

It was a full week after Larry Dominique had been captured before Montrose could carry out his instructions to take the two younger girls.

Hetty and Sydney exited out the school doors to find their rickshaw waiting for them as usual. As they started to climb in the vehicle, Hetty realized it was a different driver. She stopped, blocking Sydney from climbing in.

"Who are you?" she asked. "Where is Simon?"

"I'm Rick. I'm taking Simon's fares today. Simon's rickshaw got damaged this morning. The tricorns hauling a freight wagon got spooked and bolted. They ran right over him."

"Is he hurt?" Sydney asked.

"He's going to be lame for a couple of days," Rick said. "It's good to be cautious girls, but it's okay."

Hetty still hesitated, but she knew it was a long walk home and they both were tired. Sydney pushed past her and climbed in the seat, scooting over to leave room for her.

"C'mon, Hetty get in. I don't want to walk home."

Hetty glared at her sister, but short of dragging Sydney out of the rickshaw, she had no choice. She got in beside her.

As soon as they were out of sight of the school, Rick speeded up and turned down a different road.

"Hey!" Hetty yelled. "You're going the wrong way!"

When he ignored her, Hetty was alarmed. She grabbed her sister's arm. "Get ready to jump when I say so."

"Why? We could get hurt. Wait until he stops," Sydney protested.

"We'll have a better chance to get away if we jump out," Hetty snapped. "Just do it Sydney!"

She stood up in the now wildly rocking vehicle and jumped, dragging Sydney with her. They ended up in a tumbled heap on the road and Sydney gave a cry of pain. Rick stopped, dropped the rickshaw handles and started toward them.

"You shouldn't have done that," he said. All trace of the nice guy he had presented to them was gone.

Hetty pulled Sydney to her feet and tried to run. Sydney was crying and she was limping. Realizing they couldn't outrun him, Hetty whirled around, pushing Sydney behind her.

When he grabbed her, she kicked him hard in the shin and bit down on his arm.

"You little brat!" he yelled, and smacked her in the face, bloodying her lip.

"That wasn't necessary Rick," a man's voice said. "I have her sister. She isn't going to run off without her, are you Miss Dominique?"

Hetty looked over her shoulder. The man who spoke was a slim, blond-haired man in a new suit. He was holding Sydney by the arm. Behind him was a carriage drawn by a pair of grey tricorns.

"If you know our name, you know our sister works for the Enforcers. They'll come after you if you take us anywhere," Hetty said. She didn't think the threat would make this pair let them go, but she tried anyway.

The blond man laughed. "I'm counting on it," he said. "Put them in the carriage."

The blond picked up Sydney and deposited her on the carriage seat. He stepped back and gestured. "Well," he asked Hetty.

She jerked her arm out of Rick's grasp

and joined Sydney in the carriage.

"Did you leave the note where it could be found?" he asked.

"Yes," Rick replied. "I pinned it to the shirt of the driver, and I left him just off the road from the school. When they find him, they should find it."

Montrose frowned. "Is he alive?"

Rick shrugged. "He was when I left him."

"That's sloppy work, Rick. You should have made sure."

"Sure he was dead or sure he was alive?" Rick asked.

Montrose grunted. If Simon could describe Rick, the Enforcers would soon have his name and when they caught Rick, he would talk. Fisher wouldn't like it. As soon as this was over, he would have to dispose of Rick.

"I can't be gone too long. Drive the girls out to the Delta House and wait for me. I'll bring out some food for tonight and tomorrow."

"You mean I have to babysit those brats all night?"

"Yes. And make sure they are in good shape in the morning. The boss doesn't want them hurt."

Scowling, Rick mounted the driver's seat and drove off.

When the girls didn't arrive home that afternoon, Giselle got worried.

"What do you suppose could have happened?" she asked Henry. "The school didn't have any afterschool activities planned for today."

"Send a message to the Enforcer office," he said. "I'll follow the road to school. Maybe they just had an accident or something."

Henry didn't find the girls. He did find Simon unconscious by the side of the road. He was alive, but just barely. He had been dealt a terrific blow to his head. Henry found the note pinned to the front of his shirt when he was checking Simon for more injuries.

He unfolded it and read it, his mouth hardening as he did so. Carefully, he refolded it and put it in his pocket.

A pleasant faced man on a piebald tricorn was riding by as Henry stood up.

"Hello," the man said. "It's Henry isn't it? We met at the church social. My name is John Reynolds. Is something wrong?"

Henry nodded. "Yes. Our girls didn't come home from school this afternoon. I was back trailing them when I found him. This is the Rickshaw driver we employ to take them to and from school. He's hurt bad. Can you fetch a doctor? I don't want to move him, but I don't want to leave him either. He might wake up and say who did this."

Henry's new friend did more than summon a doctor. He also sent a message to the Sheriff's office and organized all the neighbors to search for the girls. By the time Caleb and Hercule arrived with a grim-faced Chloe and a white-faced Francis, the searchers had found the abandoned Rickshaw.

"School let out at least two hours ago," Melody said. "Whoever took them has had time to get out of the area. You should go home and wait for a ransom note."

"Yes," Henry agreed. "We'll do it. He rounded up the small group from the Enforcer's office with his eyes and set off at a brisk lope.

He was dismounting in front of the house just as the others rode up.

"Feed and water the tricorns and the dogs," Henry told Tom.

"What is it? What's happened?" Lila cried.

"Hetty and Sydney have been taken," Francis told her.

Lila screamed and collapsed into a chair. "No, No, No," she cried, bursting into tears. "What will become of me?"

Francis stared at her. "This isn't about you," she forced herself to speak

calmly. "This is about Hetty and Sydney."

When her sister continued to wail, Francis went over to a decorative table holding a vase of flowers and calmly pulled the flowers out and set them on the table. To Hercule's strangled amusement, she poured the water over her sister's head.

Lila gasped, and looked up indignantly. "You didn't have to do that."

"Shut your mouth," Francis said, fiercely. "If you can't think of anything constructive to do, just shut up."

"Have you gotten any communication from the kidnappers?" asked Hercule.

"You've got something," Caleb said to Henry. "What is it?"

Henry pulled the ransom note out of his pocket and handed it to him. "The kidnappers left this pinned to Simon's shirt."

"What do they want?" Francis asked. "My sisters and I aren't rich enough to pay ransom."

"They don't want money," Henry said. "They want Caleb, Hercule and Chloe."

"What?" Giselle exclaimed.

Caleb nodded. "We're to come alone and unarmed to the house in the delta where you were kept when they kidnapped Chloe and Giselle before."

"How much time do we have?" Chloe asked.

"They want us there by sundown, so we need to get moving pretty soon."

"You aren't going to just turn yourselves over to them?" Giselle asked.

"Chloe, Hercule and I will do exactly that," Caleb replied. "Henry, I want you and the dogs to follow us and keep out of sight."

"I'm coming with him," Francis said. "They're my sisters. I have a right to be there."

Caleb opened his mouth to forbid it, and shut it when he saw the stubborn expression on Francis' face.

"Alright," he said. "but you need different clothes. Wear something dark to blend in with the trees."

"I need to change also," Chloe announced. "Come on Francis, I'll help you pick something out."

When the girls came back down the stairs, Francis had changed into a dark rust colored shirt and pants.

"Will this do?" she asked.

"Yes, it should be fine," Hercule said.

Caleb was staring at Chloe, open mouthed. "What the Hell kind of outfit is that?" he demanded.

Giselle bit her lip to keep the chuckle

rising in her throat in check. Chloe had put on a pair of tight pants and an equally tight leather vest over a low-cut blouse. She had added thick copper bracelets studded with small metal balls. She had put her hair up under a leather hat. The hairstyle was deceptive. She had embedded some small throwing stars into each thick strand of hair and her Shū dāo (comb knife) was securely place for easy reach. The hat had been secured with long, sharp hat pins.

"You can't wear that!" Caleb exclaimed. "It's an open invitation to rape! Are you out of your mind?"

"Don't be such a prude," Chloe told him. "These clothes will ensure any male kidnappers look where I want them to and not at my hands." She shrugged, "My methods require I get close to whoever searches me. If he gets close enough to me to put hands on me, he's dead meat. It will be up to you and Hercule to take out anyone else there." She added, "This is what I do Caleb. This is who I am."

He glared at her for a moment longer, and gave in. "Alright. Is everyone ready? Then let's go."

The three of them set off for the house in the delta, alternately walking and loping the tricorns. Henry and Francis waited about ten minutes before following them.

Dusk was falling just as they arrived at the house. Rick opened the door when they mounted the stoop.

As Chloe had predicted, his eyes kept straying to the expanse of white flesh above the bustier. Rick followed them into a brightly lit living room. Hetty and Sydney were sitting on the floor in a corner. Montrose lounged against the arm of the ratty looking couch, with a drawn gun in his hand. When she saw Chloe and the others, Hetty jumped up. "It's a trap! Run!" she cried.

"Shut up," Montrose told her, waving the gun at her. Hetty said nothing else but she pulled Sydney to her feet, waiting for a chance to run themselves. If they got away, they couldn't be used as hostages.

Montrose turned to his henchman. "Did you search them for weapons?"

"Not yet," Rick admitted.

"Then do it!" Montrose snapped.

When Rick came over to search her, Chloe obligingly lifted her hands and put them behind her head. The action made her breast rise and Rick was so busy enjoying the sight presented, he didn't notice when she detached one of the small balls from her bracelet. The balls weren't metal, they were glass, painted to look metal and they were filled with pepper powder.

When Rick ran his hands down her sides and reached for her breast, she smashed one of the little balls against his cheek and it broke, coating his face and eyes with pepper powder. She had closed own her eyes and held her breath when she smashed the ball, but some of the residue still ended up on her.

He screamed, "My eyes! The bitch blinded me!" He struck out with his free hand. Half blinded by her own powder, Chloe grabbed his wrist and hung on while she drove her sharp Shū dāo through his jugular. When she pulled it out, blood spurted everywhere.

Montrose, distracted by Rick's scream and the blood, didn't see Caleb's dive coming. The two of them ended up in the floor with Montrose on the bottom. The gun went sliding across the floor.

Caleb was skilled at this type of root hog or die fighting, but so was Montrose. He bit, clawed, kicked and punched with the ferocity of a man fighting for his life. The two men rolled around on the floor, breaking tables and any other furniture in the way.

Hercule stepped around the fight and went over to the two girls. "Who hit you?" he asked Hetty, looking at her split lip.

"He did," she replied pointing at Rick.

"It's a good thing he's dead," Hercule said.

"Find some water," he told Sydney, "so Chloe can rinse the pepper out of her eyes and your sister can put a cold compress on her lip."

Sydney went to the sink and worked the hand pump, filling a bowl she found in the cabinet with cold well water.

By the time Chloe could see properly again, it was obvious the taller and heavier Caleb was winning the fight. She wiped her eyes one last time and laid the sopping cloth on the kitchen counter.

Caleb finished off Montrose with one last blow to the side of his head. Montrose slumped down, and Hercule was able to roll the man on his stomach and fasten restraints on his wrists.

Chloe brought over the bowl of water to clean the blood off Caleb's face and hands.

"Did he hurt you?" she asked.

"Yes," he replied. "He's a damn good fighter, but I beat him."

Henry and Francis arrived at the house and seeing Caleb sitting on the floor while Chloe bathed his face, they rushed inside.

Hetty and Sydney threw themselves at Francis, both crying and talking excitedly about the fight and the kidnapping.

As it had been agreed earlier, Giselle had waited about an hour before notifying Sheriff Melody she had received the ransom note. A furious Melody arrived at the house trailed by Deputy Cortez, who asked to see Lila. When she came downstairs, she threw herself into his arms and burst into tears on his shoulder.

"Why wasn't I told about this?" Melody demanded of Giselle, waving the note in frustration.

"Because we didn't want interference," she responded coolly. "It wasn't as if we ignored the law; Caleb and Hercule are both Enforcers. I suggest you follow them to the exchange point and arrest whomever they've taken into custody."

Melody breathed heavily through his nose. "I'll do that," he said. "Cortez! We're leaving."

Raymond detached Lila's clinging arms and handed her over to Giselle. "Don't worry," he assured her. "We'll get your sisters back."

When they left the house, they found Doimer waiting for them.

"Is it okay if I come with you?" he asked. "We heard at the paper you found the kidnapped girls."

"How the Hell did the Tribune learn about this?" Melody demanded.

Doimer smiled. "We have our sources,"

he said.

Melody snorted, telling himself again that this time he was going to find out who the paper's contact in the department was and ream whoever it was a new one.

"You may as well come," he told Doimer grudgingly. "You'll have to wait until my people have cleared the crime scene before you can take your photos though."

The forty-minute ride out to the Delta house gave Melody time to rein in his temper. When he and Cortez arrived, he wasn't happy to find one kidnapper dead, but he took charge of the prisoner.

"I'll expect to see all of you in the office tomorrow to make a statement," he told the Enforcers. "I'm sorry, but these young ladies will need to come in and make a statement as well."

## A RUSTY RAZOR

THE DAY AFTER the girls' ordeal, the family was sitting down to lunch when Tom reported the reporters were hanging around the front gate again.

Giselle helped herself to a few baked tubers before turning the Lazy Susan in the middle of the table so Caleb, who was sitting beside her could do the same. "This is getting annoying," she said. "Do you know one of them actually climbed over the wall this morning?"

"I can talk to them for you," offered Deputy Cortez, who had been invited to lunch in the hope of keeping Lila diverted enough to ignore the new storm of publicity.

"Turn Caleb's dogs loose in the yard," suggested Chloe. "I can guarantee they will discourage trespassers."

"I brought them with me today," Caleb said, rising. "Why don't I do that now?"

"Sit down and eat lunch first," Giselle replied.

Caleb sat back down. "Is Montrose still keeping mum?" he asked Cortez.

"Yes," Raymond replied. "It puts us in a hole as far as catching his boss goes. Without his testimony we have no proof Fisher was behind the kidnapping."

"So he's going to get away with

terrorizing my sisters?" demanded Francis.

"It looks that way. I don't blame Melody for sitting tight," Hercule put in. "Attempting to bring charges against Fisher with nothing but our suspicions would be useless, and it would tip him off we suspect him."

"It's true Montrose worked for Councilman Fisher, but he says Montrose was acting on his own, and we can't prove he wasn't."

"What about Father's diary?" Francis asked. "Didn't you say he had notes about Adams?"

"The notes don't name the client who ordered his death," Hercule stated. "Without a name to back up the accusation, we're stuck."

Giselle sighed. "I suppose we'll need to keep the girl's home from school for a few days again too."

"Did they print those awful photos again as well?" Francis asked.

"It's worse than that," Henry said. "Apparently Doimer got pictures of all of us as we were leaving the crime scene."

"Oh Lord," Chloe said.

"Yes," Henry grinned at her. "You should see the one of you in the outfit you wore."

Chloe groaned, and Caleb laughed at

her. "I warned you not to wear it," he reminded her.

"It served its purpose," Francis told him. "Henry and I were looking in the window. Rick never saw her pull out the knife she stabbed him with."

Lila set down her glass of tea with a decided snap. "Please! Must we talk about stabbing? It's bad enough we're a daily joke in the papers without having our family's shame aired in public."

She stood up, knocking over the glass she had just set down and rushed from the room.

Her departure laid a constraint over the table making everyone feel guilty about upsetting her again.

Cortez stood up. "I'll go after her. Maybe I can calm her down."

"Finish your meal first," Giselle said calmly. "She'll be much easier to soothe after she's had a good cry."

Sydney looked troubled. "Did we do something bad?"

"No, honey you didn't," Giselle said. "You girls didn't ask to be kidnapped, and you aren't responsible for whatever your father did."

"Why is Lila so upset about us getting in the paper?" Sydney persisted.

"Because she's a silly goose," Francis

said firmly. "Mother gave her the idea no one would marry us if we caused a scandal, and to Lila that's the most important thing there is."

She looked over at Giselle. "I'm sorry about this. Please don't think badly of her. We all had our methods to divert Mother when she pressured us to do something we didn't want to. I'm afraid this type of hysterical fit was Lila's. She doesn't know any other way to react when she gets into an intolerable situation. I promise I'll get her out of your hair as soon as I find a job to earn some money."

"Oh, take the stick out of your rump girl," Giselle said rudely. "If I didn't want you girls here, I would have found some way to remove you. I can deal with Lila's fits."

"I don't want to get married," Hetty announced, breaking the tension. "I want to work like you and Chloe do."

"One doesn't preclude the other," Giselle told her. "A lot of married women work to help support their families."

"I know," Hetty said in a long-suffering voice, "stay in school and learn something useful."

Francis rose from the table. "I suppose I'd better go and check on Lila," she said with resignation. "She's probably in her

room."

Several minutes later, she came down, rather pale, with a tearstained letter in her hand. "Did anyone see Lila go out?"

Giselle held out her hand for the letter, after scanning through it, she wadded it up and dropped it on the table. "Of all the melodramatic—stupid—I suppose we'd better mount a search for her."

Chloe picked up the letter and smoothed it out. "Would she do this?" she asked. "Throw herself in the river?"

"What?" Caleb exclaimed. "Let me see that!" he grabbed it out of Chloe's hand.

"I hope not, but after all this, I'm not sure what she will do," Francis admitted.

"Let's go check the river," Caleb said. "We'll take the tricorns. We should be able to overtake her before she does anything silly."

Cortez had already left. His tricorn had been tied to the hitching post out front. He set off at a quick canter, taking the shortest way to the riverbank at the edge of town.

He saw Lila standing at the edge of the water, looking down into it, and spurred his mount into a gallop. Just as she started to step off the bank into the rushing water, he snatched her up on his tricorn. The pair of them and their unwilling passenger landed belly deep into the slow-moving river.

"Why did you stop me?" Lila cried, beating on his shoulder with her fist. "Who wants to marry a girl whose father is a killer? I'm going to end up an old maid!"

He rode the saturated tricorn downstream to a shallow ford, and climbed up the bank.

"I'm not letting you kill yourself over something so silly," he informed her, giving her a shake. "If you try this again, I'll turn you over my knee."

"But—" she started.

"Shut up," Raymond said rudely. "I can tell you right now you have one offer of marriage you can be sure of, and it's mine. But I'm not going to propose until you convince me I'm not a last resort. You hear me?"

They were interrupted by the arrival of Henry, Caleb, Hercule, Frances and Chloe who charged up to them, all talking at once.

"You found her!" Caleb said.

"Is she hurt?" asked Chloe and Francis at the same time.

"She looks ok to me," Hercule observed.

"Lila? Are you alright?" Francis asked again.

Raymond gave Lila another shake.

"Answer your sister. You've frightened everyone enough for one day."

Lila cast an angry look up into his face. "Yes, Francis. I'm fine. I just need some dry clothes."

"Let's get you home so you can change," Chloe said.

Lila sulked all the way back to the house. It wasn't until her two little sisters burst into tears at the sight of her that guilt hit her.

"Please don't die," Sydney wailed, clinging to her.

"We just lost Mamma and Papa," Hetty said, gulping back tears. "We don't want to lose you too."

Lila looked over their heads at Francis, encountering an angry stare.

"I'm sorry," she whispered. "I didn't think—just—it would be better if I wasn't here."

"You mean you didn't think about anyone but yourself," Francis said brutally.

"Hey!" Raymond said. "She said she was sorry. It's over now. You should let it go."

He flushed a little under Lila's grateful smile.

Francis sighed. Being angry wouldn't change Lila into a person she wasn't; she had to let it go. "We need to get you into

some dry clothes," she said.

When she came back downstairs after putting Lila to bed, she found Hercule in the hall getting ready to leave.

"You're quite a gal, Francis Dominque," he said. "Aunt Hortense would love you. You would have made a good Jones woman."

"Thank you, I think," she said, watching his tall figure as he rode away. Who was Aunt Hortense?

## EVIL AS EVIL CAN BE

THE TRIAL of Gavin Montrose for the kidnapping of the two Dominique sisters was scheduled for a Tuesday morning. Francis and Chloe brought the younger girls with them to work the day of the trial.

"We can leave for the courthouse from the Enforcer's office," Chloe said. "I see no reason for us to be at the courthouse before Montrose arrives. The trial can't start until he's present in court."

"If we arrive when he does, all the media attention will be focused on him and we can slip into the courthouse without those nosy reporters harassing the girls about what happened," Francis agreed.

They were out back, saddling the tricorns for the trip to the courthouse when a single shot rang out, followed by a cascade of more guns going off.

"Stay here!" Chloe told Francis and the girls. Drawing her gun, she ran around the side of the building. Montrose's body lay sprawled on the steps of the sheriff's office with a bloody hole in the center of his chest.

Her eyes sought Caleb first and she breathed a sigh of relief when she found him alive. He and Hercule were crouched

behind the water trough in the center of the street, guns drawn, their eyes scanning the rooftops across from the sheriff's office.

Chloe stood up, keeping her back to the building. A professional sniper wouldn't stick around once his kill was made. He would leave the area and the best way to do it without being seen was out the back of whatever building he had used for the shot.

She turned and went back to Francis and the girls. "Go back inside," she said. "We won't be needed to testify today. Montrose is dead." She looked at Caleb's head groom. "Go with them, Bill. I'll take Athena with me."

"What are you going to do Miss?" he asked frowning.

"The sniper is going to come out the back of one of the empty buildings on this side of the street. I'm going to look for him."

When she unfastened the latch on Athena's kennel, the dog looked up eagerly. The scar from the bullet on the top her head was still a little red, but it was healing nicely.

"Ready for some action?" Chloe murmured, and Athena gave a soft woof! In reply.

Unless he was still hiding in the

buildings, which to her trained assassin's mind, would have been extremely foolish, the sniper was long gone, but it would be equally foolish not to check out the two empty buildings on this side of the street.

She peered around the back corner of the stable, looking for a plume of dust to mark the sniper's exit. It was a hot day and there had been no rain for several weeks. If the sniper ran after he shot there should have been some dust raised; if he had been smart enough to move slowly though, he might not have stirred up enough dust for a trail of it to be seen.

Chloe stood up frowning. She had waited too long; the faint plume of dust rising toward the affluent district might be the sniper, but it could just as easily be an innocent traveler.

Keeping close to the back of the buildings, she made her way to the back door of the first empty shop. The door was standing half open. She signaled Athena for a quiet search and the huge dog slipped silently through the door, Chloe followed her. In silent hunt mode, Athena wouldn't bark unless she found someone.

This building had once housed a feed and grain store. It smelled faintly of dust, dried oats and rodents. A few empty grain bins had been left in the store and she used them for cover as she checked out the room. She didn't expect to find anyone still hiding out down here; had she been planning the kill she would have set up on the roof or in one of the upper story rooms giving the best line of sight to the jail steps.

Athena returned without signaling she had found anyone. Still, it was better to be careful than surprised, so Chloe methodically checked the downstairs area before starting up the stairs. She again sent Athena ahead of her in stealth mode.

Chloe kept as close to the wall as she could when ascending the darkened stairway, both to lessen the chance the stairs would squeak and give her presence away as to make it difficult to spot her.

The rooms on the second floor were empty also, but she did find the sniper's nest in one of the bedrooms. She could see marks in the dust where a comfortable chair from the living room had been dragged into this room. Doubtless so the sniper could wait in comfort while watching the jail. A few spent shell casings were lying under the open window.

She stood up and looked out the window, being careful not to show herself; she didn't want to get accidentally shot by any nervous deputies.

Taking a cloth bag out of her pouch,

she used a splinter of wood to rake the shell casings into it. With any luck the dogs could get a scent to follow off the shells, which had most certainly been handled by the sniper.

She called Athena to follow and went back down the stairs. She entered the Enforcer office through the kitchen. She found the girls, Francis and Bill anxiously waiting in the reception office.

"He's gone," she reported. She went to the door and stepped out onto the porch. "He's gone," she called to Caleb and Hercule, who stood up and came towards her.

"Are you sure?" Caleb asked.

"Yes. Athena and I found his nest in an empty grain store." She pulled the bag out of her pouch and held it out. "I picked up some shell casings from there. Maybe the dogs can take a scent from it and follow whoever did it."

## THE STARS RUSH OUT

CHLOE WOKE THE day after Montrose had been killed and lay there for a while, listening to the birdsong outside her window. She heard Kimi brushing sand in the litter box and smelled a brief whiff of fresh Fox poop. She smelled it again when Rakki imitated his mother and used it too. She would have to ask Mary to change the sand today.

The glow preceding the rising sun gave light to the room. Chloe rose and dressed in the loose clothing she wore for her morning workouts. Kimi and Rakki followed her down the stairs, the kit doing a tumble the last few steps and ending up splayed on the floor. Chloe bent and rubbed his back consolingly. "Keep trying," she said. "You'll get it right."

Francis jumped a little when Chloe entered the kitchen. "Oh, I didn't realize anyone else was up," she said.

"Kimi woke me up," Chloe yawned. "Nothing like a good whiff of fresh Fox pee to bring you awake. Is there coffee?"

"Yes, I just made some. It should be done by now." Francis took two mugs out of the cupboard and poured the dark rich coffee into them. She handed one to Chloe.

"Let's sit outside and watch the sun come up," Chloe suggested.

The garden air was still cool from the night as the two girls settled themselves at the table under a tree. Kimi and Rakki investigated the smells under a nearby bush.

Francis yawned. "See what you started," she said. "Yawning is catching."

Chloe sipped her coffee, using both hands to hold the cup. "How is Lila?" she asked.

Francis shrugged. "She seems better. Raymond telling her she was acting the fool seems to have done much more to bring her back to herself than anything Giselle or I said to her. Maybe we've been pampering her too much."

Chloe took another sip of the hot liquid. "Do you think she will marry him?"

"Yes," Francis answered. "If he proposes. Did you know he told her he wouldn't marry her until she convinced him she wasn't marrying him as a last resort?"

Chloe chuckled. "I didn't hear about it. When did he tell her that?"

"The day he stopped her jumping in the river. She asked me how she could convince him she loves him. Can you imagine? Asking me of all people. I've never even had a gentleman friend."

"You do alright," Chloe said. "Some men appreciate a woman who can stand beside them rather than one who has to be shielded from trouble. Francis, your kind of woman is the one who stands up beside her man. Lila is the other."

Francis smiled wryly. "Maybe. Anyone I marry would have to be willing to take Hetty and Sydney as well."

"If Lila marries Deputy Cortez, perhaps they could live with them."

"No," Francis said. "Hetty would end up a drudge running the house for Lila and Sydney would never become the artist I know she can be."

Francis sipped her own coffee, eyeing Chloe speculatively.

"What about you? I think Caleb cares a lot about you. I can see it when he looks at you."

"I hope he does, but there are some things he doesn't know about me; about what I used to do. I don't know if finding them out will change how he feels."

Francis looked at her curiously. "What things?"

"I wasn't always an investigator," Chloe said. "My mother trained me to kill as well as investigate. I was involved in one of the cases in Azure City he's been looking into."

"Involved?"

"The man who died was a bad man, and he was going to try and kill Giselle's family

so he could take their ranch and mine. He had already crippled her son. The local Women's Circle requested I remove the threat. So I did."

"Does Caleb know you killed him?"

"He let me read through his notes on the case. I think he suspects it," Chloe admitted.

"What are you going to do?" Francis asked.

"I can't live with this hanging over me; I have to talk to him about it."

She set her cup down on the table and moved over to the smooth area she used for her morning exercises. Francis joined her, and a few moments later, so did Hetty.

"Where's Sydney?" Francis asked.

Hetty shrugged. "She rolled over and put her pillow over her head when I tried to wake her up. She stayed up late last night working on a painting."

Francis frowned; Sydney had real artistic talent, but she wanted both the girls to be able to defend themselves and she knew it wouldn't happen if they were stuck working on the beginning moves.

"Let her be, Francis," Chloe said. "She won't get anything out of the exercises unless she wants to do them."

After breakfast, while Francis busied herself getting her younger sisters off to school, Chloe presented her findings about Adams murder to her client.

Grace had barely sat down on one of the parlor chairs when she asked, "I got your message. Did you find out who murdered my brother-in-law?"

"Yes," Chloe said. "Well, I know who did the actual deed, and he's in custody."

"Who did it?"

"A man named Larry Dominique did the actual killing."

Grace frowned, casting a glance at Francis who had rejoined them after watching her sisters ride their tricorns out the gate accompanied by Henry. "Isn't he your father?"

"Yes," Francis said. "Neither my mother or any of us had any idea he was other than a bookkeeper with itchy feet until the Enforcers and the Sheriff found his murder diary."

"But he's been arrested?"

"Yes," Chloe said. "However, In addition to his bookkeeping business, Larry Dominique was also a killer for hire. According to the diary, Samuel Adams' killing was paid for by another person."

"Who hated him enough to kill him?"

"The diary doesn't say. Dominique used initials to identify his clients, and

while I do think I know who the initials might belong to, I have no proof, and at this point it doesn't look as though we will get any."

"I see," Grace said slowly. "It wasn't my sister who paid for it?"

"No, I can say for sure your sister didn't do it or hire it, and neither of you is in any danger from the person we think hired the killing."

"How can you be so sure?" Grace demanded.

"Samuel Adams was murdered because he was dipping his wick in the wrong man's candle," Chloe said bluntly.

"You mean a jealous husband had him killed?"

Chloe nodded. "That's right. The husband has no reason to come after either your sister or you."

Grace Trevelyan nodded. "Thank you for finding out who did it." She wasn't completely satisfied, but she paid her bill and left.

Francis looked over at Chloe. "I thought she would be more insistent about knowing who ordered him killed, but she only asked about it once, and you didn't actually tell her who we think it was. Why did she let it drop?"

"I'm not sure," Chloe said, "but I always wondered how Fisher found out about the affair. Susan Fisher didn't tell anyone, and I don't think Adams would have told either. At least not about Councilman Fisher's wife."

"You think Grace told Fisher? Why would she?"

"She did have a motive to get rid of him," Chloe said. "She is half owner of the store, remember? If he was using it as a base for a criminal enterprise, she could have lost any income from it if he got caught."

"That's diabolical," Francis exclaimed.

Chloe smiled wryly. "Motives for murder can be complicated. Grace might not have wanted him dead, just out of the picture."

"But she asked you to find out who killed him. I don't understand why she would want you to investigate his murder if she set it up."

"So she could keep an eye on the investigation."

When Chloe and Francis arrived at the Enforcer's office later, they found Hercule talking to a young man with shaggy blond hair and a neat mustache.

"Just apply for a job down at City Hall," Hercule was saying. "I know Fisher needs a new clerk, so probably you'll get hired immediately."

"We'll use a dead drop at the feed store

for reports and messages."

"What is a dead drop?" Francis asked, causing both men to jump.

"Oh, it's you Francis," Hercule said. "I didn't hear you come in."

"It's called a dead drop when one person leaves a message in a certain place and another person picks it up without it appearing they've met," Chloe explained.

Hercule nodded agreement. "Francis, Chloe this is Jared Blackman. He's out of the Enforcers office in Gateway. You don't know him, and you've never met him."

"Nice to not meet you, Mr. Blackman," Francis said. And Blackman grinned.

"The same to you, Ladies." He turned to Hercule. "I'll go out the back way."

Francis sat down at the reception desk and went through the handwritten notes she was supposed to type up.

"Is Caleb in his office?" Chloe asked.

"Yes," Hercule said. "I think he's writing up his notes for the prostitute killings to be sent to the main office."

Chloe nodded and went in, shutting the door behind her before sitting down across the desk from Caleb.

His eyebrows rose when he saw the closed door. "Something you want to say privately?"

"Yes," she said. She laid a sheaf of

paper down on the desk between them. "I read your notes on the Johnson killing."

He watched her gravely, waiting for her to go on.

"You know who killed him don't you?"

"I think so, yes."

He waited.

"What do you intend to do about it?" she blurted out. "Are you going to arrest me?"

"No," he shook his head. "It's not because of how I feel about you, it's because I know what it is to be beholden to a family or a group of people and to need to kill someone who threatens them. Johnson was a bad egg. He would have been a continued threat to a lot of good people. He had plans for the deaths of at least five others. Killing him stopped that. It's a question of balancing their lives against his."

He held out his hand, and when Chloe put hers into it, he pulled her up into his arms. They stood there for a few minutes, before he tilted her chin up so he could kiss her.

"I've just sent Blackman off to get a job in Fisher's office," Hercule announced, opening the door. "Whoops! I didn't mean to interrupt anything."

He and Francis stood there in the doorway, grinning at them.

GAIL DALEY

"You can be the first to congratulate us," Caleb told them. "We're going to be married."

## ST. ANTONI HISTORICAL NOTES

WHEN THE technology to locate and open gates to other worlds was discovered on Earth in the late 21st century, access to this knowledge was tightly guarded by government and industry hoping to exploit the vast resources on these new worlds. The Portal Settlement Act made it a crime to open a gate or emigrate through a portal to any world not released for settlement by the United Earth Government. It took relatively little energy to power up a gate made taking advantage of these new worlds doubly attractive to government and industry. To ensure the legal outposts thrived, Settlers on Earth 's approved colonies received the best in technology and supplies available. The sanctioned colonies also had the militaries of Earth to prevent anarchy.

Despite government's tight control, the knowledge it was possible to open a doorway to other worlds couldn't be kept secret. The Portal technology was leaked, and unregulated gates popped up like fleas on a dog in summer. These Colonies came to be called "the Forbidden Colonies". Of which St. Antoni was one of many. Immigrants who reached St. Antoni were desperate to escape Earth . St. Antoni was named for an early settler's fondness for a little jingle that goes like this: "St. Antoni, please look around—something is lost and must be found." Being a maverick at heart, he changed the spelling of Saint Anthony in the original rhyme to suit himself.

Immigrants who snuck in through illegal Portals only had the supplies and technology they could carry to build their new life on a new world. They depended on their wits, ingenuity and sheer cussedness to defend themselves against the alien plants and bizarre animals found on the new worlds. But they came because of man's lust to explore and because they wanted freedom and adventure. Unlike citizens of officially recognized colonies, who had the powerful Earth government and industry to help them build homes and plant crops for food, immigrants to the forbidden colonies like St. Antoni had to do the same under more primitive conditions With intelligence, courage, and determination, they built a new society on a new world. In the first two hundred years they created a civilization as different from Earth as Mars is from Venus. City states were controlled by powerful families or groups, and the outlying ranches and mines outside them were held together like medieval baronies by guns and guts.

The new citizens of St. Antoni found

themselves dumped on a primitive world; there was no law to protect the new colonists from each other and for a time anarchy and lawlessness ruled. In due course and after many bloody battles, a system of government loosely based on what had been used in the mining districts and cattle associations popular in the early nineteenth century, with a smattering of that found in feudal medieval societies. These regulations were enforced by Peacekeepers inside the City States.

Each of the Seven City States was run by a single family or a group of individuals who seized power during periods of civil disturbance. While most of the ruling families gave lip service to electing councils with representatives to make major decisions, somehow it always happened that those elected were related to or owed allegiance to the family who held the power in that state. Regulations passed by these councils were enforced inside areas claimed by each City State.

A similar set of laws, based on those passed by each City State, held sway inside the smaller towns around them. These laws were enforced by locally elected sheriffs and passed by town councils. Outlying ranches and mines, much like the feudal barons in Earth history, kept their own armed retainers to ensure the safety of the workers and families living on or around them.

A loose agreement between the City States authorized roving marshals to track down lawbreakers in the wilderness areas between them. Although theoretically independent of control by any one City State, District Marshals were paid out of tithes collected by the city nearest them.

But the St. Antonoians new civilization had a flaw: a man or woman could commit crimes in one City state flee to another and be safe from pursuit. To combat this flaw, the Enforcers were created to supplement the District Marshals. Only this group of brave men and women, an elite law enforcement agency commissioned by the combined city states, dares to pursue outlaws across the borders. When they catch up with them, they serve as judge, jury and sometimes executioners...

On some illegally opened worlds, the new communities failed miserably, but others like St. Antoni, thrived. It was the luck of the draw the illicit portal opened onto a planet closely resembling its parent world. St. Antoni possessed a yellow sun, darker than the one shining on Earth , but it looked down on blue seas, land masses covered with lush grass, gray Ironwood forests, high snowy mountains, hot dry deserts and continents threaded by

large rivers and small streams. Plants and animals had developed along lines genetically close enough to Earth to support human life, and St. Antoni's temperature range was close enough to Earth to make living there bearable for humans.

Civilization on St. Antoni succeeded where some of the others didn't, because of a few lucky conditions. The animal and plant life on St. Antoni was compatible with humans and could support human life. Native plants readily adapted to being farmed, and cuttings and seedlings the settlers brought with them thrived and grew in the new soil. A native cotton-like plant was discovered and harvested for clothing in the warmer climates. Native grains were adapted to make bread, and even some beans and leafy plants were harvested as substitutes for Coffee and tea.

## TECHNOLOGY

TECHNOLOGY levels in the forbidden colony worlds differed, but in all of them a rich trade in books, diagrams, information and other needed items flourished. On St. Antoni, these items were brought in by daring Portal Runners who made the perilous trip back and forth to Earth, risking discovery and imprisonment. Of

course, a Runner didn't perform this service for free. A Portal Runner making the dangerous trip to smuggle in people and technology charged a high price for the service.

Like most of the other illegally opened worlds, St. Antonians maintained their semi-modern lifestyle by using technology not requiring massive amounts of electrical power or massive factories. The discovery of Bluestones, a mineral when mixed with water produced heat and steam, made it practical for St. Antonians to build a variety of steam engines to power lights, refrigeration units, cookstoves, steamboats and even a steam engine driven train. Mines and foundries were developed to excavate the metals needed for these endeavors.

By sheer grit and determination St. Antonians fought their way to the steam age. Settlers who could afford them had steam operated generators for their homes and businesses to provide light, heat and other comforts.

Settlers were spreading out over the single continent where the original gateway had opened, and ships were exploring the seas. Steamboats plied the waterways and a railroad system allowed for travel between the City States. It was rumored someone had brought through a copy of the Tesla theory and experiments were being done to build a Tesla Generator.

The industries developed by the settlers, were mostly farming, ranching and mining in the interior, and fishing along the coastal areas, although manufacturing was growing. Travel took the form of steamboats along the deep rivers, and a newly built railroad system connecting the largest City states using steam driven trains. To get to anywhere else, the settlers walked, rode or drove a tricorn pulled wagon.

## POLITICAL STRUCTURE

ST. ANTHONI'S illegally founded portal in Gateway City had been open for several hundred years, giving its settlers time to develop seven City States with loosely connected governments. Except for areas directly connecting the City States, much of St. Antoni was still wild and unexplored. In the years the St. Antoni gateway had been open, Portal Runners had brought in a steady trickle of new settlers and other items highly valued on a planet without its own technological resources.

The area around River Crossing and its companion across the river, Minerstown, was dominated by six powerful families who together controlled mining and ranching in the area. Rather than decimate their livelihoods by fighting until only one family was left standing the families of Kenefic had jointly come to an agreement to settle their differences with a joint council. The mountains above River Crossing were rich in gold, silver, bluestones and gems. The Lucky Strike, owned by Michael St. Vyr, mined Bluestone, the other mines owned by the six families, worked gold, silver and various gemstones.

## NATIVE ANIMALS

OUT OF necessity, native animals were domesticated and adapted to human use. With a few exceptions the St. Antonians tended to use familiar names for new animals whose use or physical characteristics were close to those found on Earth.

A prime example of a domesticated native animal was the **tricorn,** who ranged the valleys and plains of the new world in large herds. Named for their three horns; the animals had two spikes set high in the forehead, and a third at the end of their noses. Tricorns were herd animals, and like the horses they resembled, once domesticated, served a variety of purposes for the settlers. Tricorns resembled large horses with two slim horns on their broad forehead and a shorter one on the end of their nose. They were striped like a zebra, but the stripes came in a variety of colors; the most common being red and black. Once tamed to man's use, the settlers rode tricorns, used them to pull plows and other forms of transportation much the way their ancestors on Earth had used the horse.

Overlarge, **shaggy coated goats** were another native animal compatible with humans. About the size of a Herford cow, both sexes possessed large horns curving on the sides of their heads. Living mostly in small family groups in rocky areas, they fed on the short, dark grass growing there. Combining the purposes cows and goats had served on Earth , St. Antoni goats produced drinkable milk and edible cheeses. Their long, soft hair was sheered and collected yearly to be woven into cloth. Most goats were striped black or brown and white, enabling them to blend in with the rocks around them

Early settlers also domesticated several species of native birds for meat and eggs. Most popular was a large, rainbow-feathered bird, who made honking noises reminiscent of the **geese** they were named after.

The **cattle** caught and herded by the settlers for meat and leather, were not actually cattle but another ruminant. They

resembled a Texas longhorn cow with four horns, a long shaggy coat and a spiked tail. Like their Texas namesakes, they came with a mean disposition.

There was a species of feline dubbed **Bobcat** by the settlers who first saw them. A St. Antoni Bobcat weighed around twenty-five pounds, with a short-haired coat, a stubby tail, tuffs on the ears, and gold and black stripes. Bobcats soon adopted the human settlements as a place to find much of the small game they fed on, and it wasn't long before humans returned the favor and they became household pets.

A small mammal the size of an Earth cat but closely resembling a **fox** was also adopted as pets. They had four legs, a long, fluffy tail with a white tip and retractable claws. The creatures had a wedge-shaped head with a pointed nose and big eyes. Their soft, smooth skin was covered in thin red fur.

There were more unpleasant animals as well. A nasty reptile the settlers called **Sanders** lived in the hotter areas of the planet and often hid under bushes and rocks. Sanders had a venomous bite, were bright orange and closely resembled Earthly snakes.

**Dire Bears**, so called because of their enormous size and vicious dispositions, made dens in the thick pink bushes along

the rivers. Solitary omnivores, they fished the streams, ate small animals and berries, and warred with the equally large prides of grey striped lions who lived in the areas above some of the rivers. The mountains above the valleys were home to tree-climbing, spotted lupine packs whose main food were the goat herds.

## EARTH – MOTHER OF WORLDS

Earth survived the multitude of physical and social disasters leading to the apocalypse. The united States and Canada had contingencies for disasters in place but none of them had been designed for nation-wide lasting several years. The political structure, already in turmoil because of a series of pandemic viruses the authorities seemed unable to check, was near collapse.

Scientists had predicted for years that the tectonic plates holding the continents in position were due to move. No one had believed this was imminent until it happened. The Pacific Rim of Fire was the first. Massive eruptions of the volcanos making up the rim set off earthquakes along the three main fault lines running down the spine of the Americas. The global economy, already shaky because of the pandemics, worsened, crumpled in some places, and complete anarchy reigned.

North America and parts of Europe had a semblance of government still intact, albeit with some radical changes. Armed government soldiers did their best to help beleaguered police departments keep order in the large cities where gangs of loosely unified 'protesters' periodically organized marches invariably leading to rioting, looting and the destruction of businesses, homes, autos and anything else they could find.

In more rural areas, the fiercely independent citizen's militia groups protected citizens from both the spread of criminal gangs fighting for control of the cities, and the government agencies who seemed more interested in sweeping aside citizens' rights than protecting them.

Thus matters had stood when scientists discovered a way to escape to another world by opening a Portal to it. The fact that it took relatively little energy to power up a gate made taking advantage of these new worlds doubly attractive to government and industry. Prospective settlers lined up in droves to emigrate to these new world and much money was made providing access and supplies for the new colonies.

Eager to restore their crumbling economies, Earth governments and industry banded together control this knowledge, creating the Portal Settlement Acts. The Acts made it a crime to open a gate or emigrate through a portal to any world not released for settlement by the United Earth Governments. Despite attempts to regulate the information about how to make a gate, creating one didn't require a lot of scientific knowledge. Coupled with the low amount of energy required to run one, gates began springing up like fleas on a dog in summer. A mishmash of different smuggling rings, eager to supply the illicit colonies with badly needed tech, supplies and just about anything else they needed or wanted also sprang up.

An uneasy alliance developed between the smugglers and the militia, who were anti-government control, and fiercely protective of citizen's rights. These militia groups automatically resented the Portal Authority telling them where they could live.

Desperate to stop the flow of money slipping away, Earth governments used the Acts to create the Portal Authority, giving its agents powers similar to police and military to combat the smugglers and to investigate and arrest violators of the Acts. The Acts and the behavior of the first agents enforcing it created fertile ground for rebellion.

During this time an underground

railroad system developed to help citizens escape the chaos on earth. Many of those wanting to escape had reasons for emigrating not considered acceptable by the large corporations who managed the Portal Authority, or who couldn't put up the enormous amount of 'homestead stake funds' required by those who controlled the new colonies. For the most part, the underground emigration and smuggling of tech, information and other badly needed items, was usually supported by the citizen's militias; these informally organized groups were very anti-government controls and very protective of their citizen's rights and automatically resented the Portal Authority telling them where they could live.

Not everyone who hated the Portal Authority agreed the Portals should be open to all; several powerful conspiracy groups suspected opening the portals had caused the plates to shift and wanted them closed. All these agencies spied on each other and the citizens and occasional armed clashes between them kept the citizen's militia active.

Government and Industry decided to restore order to the larger population centers first, leaving the outlying small towns and rural areas to fend for themselves. When the military and national guard finally got around to the communities outside the cities, they had found armed citizens militia in control, who were not inclined to give authority back to civil governments whose fumbling they blamed for the destruction. Eventually a truce was worked out, but the Militia was still a force to be reckoned with outside the cities.

Secret Portals existed in many communities with ties to the Militia. The Portal located outside Laughing Mountain was one of these, and a local business, Delany's Fine Art & Antiques, a feature on Main Street of the small town of Laughing Mountain for more than two hundred years, was a staging point on the smuggling route. Besides doing a brisk trade in antiques and rare books, the shop was a place where Portal Runners, the name given smugglers who worked both sides of the Portal, could ship items intended for illegal colonies.

Laughing Mountain was nestled in the rolling hills of what had once been the eastern edge California's coastal mountains. The town was about an hour's drive from the rebuilt city of Carmel by the Sea. The high-priced homes of the rich and famous who lived there were slowly being rebuilt as governments regained some control of the cities. Martial Law was slowly being phased out.

The isolation of the smaller towns and settlements had helped prevent the spread of the pandemics, and communities such as Laughing Mountain had taken steps to prevent the spread of the social unrest plaguing their brethren in the larger cities. In these small rural communities, life had gone on much as usual. People worked, grew food to feed themselves and their neighbors and children attended school. No one talked about the Portal Gate outside of town, or the flow of traffic going through it each week.

Gradually, the rich and famous returned to rebuild cities along the new coastlines, bringing their money and idle lifestyles back to the areas they had abandoned. They often spent an idle afternoon shopping in the small towns up in the mountains, followed by lunch or tea at the boutique cafe's catering to their trade.

# ABOUT THE AUTHOR

GAIL DALEY is a self-taught artist and writer with a background in business. An omnivorous reader, she was inspired by her son, also a writer, to finish some of the incomplete novels she had begun over the years. She is heavily involved in local art groups and fills her time reading, writing, painting in acrylics, and spending time with her husband of 40 plus years. Currently her family is owned by two cats, a mischievous young cat called Mab (after the fairy queen of air and darkness) and a mellow Gray Princess named Moonstone. In the past, the family shared their home with many dogs, cats and a Guinea Pig, all of whom have passed over the rainbow bridge. A recent major surgery on her stomach and a bout with breast cancer has slowed her down a little, but she continues to write and paint.

# A NOTE FROM GAIL

THANK YOU for reading this book. Reviews are bread and butter to Indie authors like me, so it would be much appreciated if you write a review and share it on the site where this book was purchased.

I often get asked why I write; the answer is simple. I write books I personally would like to read. While it's always a joy to find readers who like the stories I like, I'm aware my brand of writing won't please everyone. Please write to me anyway. I'd love to hear from you.

If you would like to know when my next books are coming out, please follow me on social media sites or sign up to receive E-mail notices:

https://books2read.com/author/gail-daley/subscribe/1/72820/

E-mail lists are never shared with 3rd parties. Any notices you receive will only be from me.

# BONUS: EXCERPT FROM WARRIORS OF ST. ANTONI

## SOMETHING WICKED THIS WAY COMES

The Town of River Crossing and its sister Minerstown were in the City State of Kenefic. The area was dominated by several powerful families who together controlled mining and ranching in the area. Rather than decimate their livelihoods by fighting until only one family was left standing as had happened elsewhere, the families of Kenefic had jointly come to an agreement to settle their differences with a council consisting of a member of each family.

The mountains above River Crossing were rich in gold, silver, bluestones and gems. The Lucky Strike, owned by Michael St. Vyr, mined Bluestone, the other mines owned by the Council families, worked gold, silver and various gemstones.

Michael St. Vyr had come through the portal in Gateway City with his parents when he was a child. By the power of his own hard work and ingenuity, he had carved a place for himself and his family in the enormous valley at the base of the mountains on the northern continent. He now owned a Bluestone mine, gold, gemstone and silver claims in the hills above the valley, and a cattle and goat ranch with a good house and twenty acres of orchards.

Folks around River Crossing described him as a dangerous man to cross. He was a

big man, solid, with a mane of graying red hair. His three pretty daughters, well he thought they were pretty, had recently come home from Copper City. He was on the road leading from his ranch into town, because he had just come from a meeting with his lawyer. Michael was pleased to think he had made satisfactory arrangements to divide his property equally between his three girls and their husbands in the event of his death.

"None of your daughters are married or engaged," his lawyer, Terrance Milliner, pointed out.

St. Vyr waved that quibbling objection away. "Doesn't matter. I have plans to take care of that. Before the year is out, I plan for all three of my girls to be wed."

Riding home after signing the papers, his satisfaction was marred by an uncomfortable itch growing on the back of his neck that got worse the further away from town he rode. He knew better than to ignore the feeling.

He had been twelve the first time it happened. He and his parents followed a Portal Runner through an unregulated gate to the raw new world of St. Antoni. The emigrant camp where they were taken by the Runner was a wild place. Young Michael's family had only been in the immigrant camp three days before his father had been gunned down and robbed of the small number of gems, he had been carrying to the money changer. After Jess St. Vyr was killed, an investigation was done, but the investigator simply reported it had been a fair shooting because Jess had been armed. Michael and his mother had been left to fend for themselves in the camp.

Michaels neck itched that day too; he had been afraid of something bad happening that day and had begged his father to let him accompany him, but Jess St. Vyr had left him with his mother.

After her husband's death, Giselle, Michael's mother quickly discovered that on this new world a woman needed to be tough enough to protect herself or find someone to do it for her. A strong-minded woman, she decided to learn how to take care of herself and her son. Michael and his mother were left at the mercy of a society that expected its people to be able to protect, feed and clothe themselves on their own. His parents had been fleeing an organized gang back home, so returning to Earth on a permanent basis was out of the question. To support herself and her son, Giselle became a Portal Runner. apprenticing with the woman who brought them over. Portal Runners traveled back and forth between Earth and

St. Antoni, smuggling in goods and people. Between trips she supported them with a variety of enterprises.

His father's death had taught Michael a lesson; he never again ignored the warning he got from his gut and it saved his life many times over.

He paid heed to the warning now, and carefully examined the area around the road because paying attention to his surroundings had kept him alive a long time. He could see nothing out of place, however. The road leading from his ranch the Golden Tricorn into town was smooth; it had been recently graded by his own workers. The deep drainage ditch that kept the road from becoming a mire during the rainy season was dry. The thorn bushes growing in it would be underwater when the rains came, but that was not due to happen for several months. It was high summer and the waves of knee-high buttery grass, broken here and there with tall thorn bushes, gave the undulating landscape a deceptively flat look. Evening was drawing near and the valley was beginning to cool from the blistering heat of a summer day. Long shadows had begun to shade the road.

The road had no heavy traffic this late in the afternoon, but it was busy enough to be safe from bands of roving outlaws. Deciding he wanted a better look around,

he dismounted and fussed ostensibly with the cinch holding the saddle on his red and black striped tricorn. St. Vyr took the opportunity to loosen the gun in his holster while he was pretending to fiddle with the cinch. He never got the chance to draw it.

Without warning, a savage blow followed by the crack of a high-powered rifle hit him in the lower back. His Tricorn, Redbird, had been trained not to flinch from gunfire and stood like a rock when Michael collapsed against him. But when a second bullet burned the animal across the rump, he took off running, leaving his master to fall half in, half out of the drainage ditch.

St. Vyr slumped to the ground, still conscious but unable to feel his legs. He was lightheaded, and knew he was in danger of passing out. He touched his waist and brought his hand away red with his own blood. The light wavered in front of his eyes and he knew he had to find cover before whoever fired the shots came to see if he had killed him. Desperately, he used his powerful arms to drag himself all the way into the drainage ditch at the side of the road. He slid sideways and rolled down into it. The ditch was dry this time of year and overgrown with thorn bushes. Just before he passed out, he rolled under a bush, praying there wasn't a Sander, one of St. Antoni's poisonous reptiles, lurking under it seeking shade from the heat of the day. Michael pulled some of the dead bushes lining the ditch over himself before blacking out.

Tricorns, like the horses they had replaced, were herd animals. The stallion ran hard for a few miles before he slowed to a more moderate pace as he made his way back to the ranch. Reaching the barn, he stopped outside the corral where he had the remuda tricorns for company.

The ranch house itself was a large two-story structure built with sun baked bricks made of the local dried grasses and clay found along the riverbanks. High walls, broken apart with narrow slits for windows made from the same material, enclosed an inner courtyard. Barns and corrals for animals rested against the outside wall facing the fruit and nut orchard, and a bunkhouse for the workers attached to the other wall. Racks of Bluestones to power the ranch's steam generators were stored on layers of frames under a roof supported by long poles, so they couldn't develop moisture and catch fire. St. Antoni's first immigrants had discovered the bluestones by accident soon after they arrived. A man had spilled some water on a pile of them and they burst

into flame. His partner, an engineer, experimented with adapting the chemical reaction from the mixture of stones and water to create enough heat to run a steam engine. The first few steam generators had been made from parts smuggled in from Earth , but the engineer and his partner soon got rich making their own generators with parts made from a home-made alloy of iron, carbon, copper and tin.

Coming home several hours after Redbirds arrival at the corral, Michaels daughter Jeanne found her father's tricorn loose in front of the corrals. Annoyed, because she hadn't counted on her father being home and possibly asking her questions about what she had been doing, she was busy thinking up excuses as she rode up.

Her father had given orders that the girls weren't to ride out alone, which Jeanne had disobeyed, and not for the first time. The youngest of Michael's three daughters, she was accustomed to getting her own way by a combination of sweet cajolery or tantrums. Jeanne wasn't above using her looks ruthlessly to obtain what she wanted, but she knew her father wouldn't be fooled by the attributes that distracted others. Growing up, she had gotten away with doing forbidden things because when she was a young girl, people

were diverted by her huge blue eyes that she could make swim with tears and her quivering lips. As she grew older, men especially failed to see past the lush figure, golden hair and red-lipped mouth. They frequently missed the hard-headed intelligence peeking out of those lovely turquoise eyes.

When her father didn't appear, she dismounted and breathed a sigh of relief. She tied her gray striped mare up to the hitching rail in front of the tack room and unsaddled her. Coming out with a brush and currycomb after she deposited her saddle on a rack inside, she was surprised to see that Redbird, her father's mount had come up to the hitching rail where she had tied Grayling her own tricorn, and was investigating the feedbag she had dropped over her nose.

"Redbird, how did you get loose?" she demanded of the tricorn, picking up his trailing reins. As she moved to re-tie him to the rail, she spotted the wound, still oozing a trickle of blood, on his rump where the second bullet had grazed him. When she stepped back and looked more carefully at the stallion, she could see a smear of blood on the stirrup leather.

Her first impulse was to remount and back trail Redbird to see if she could find her father. Looking around for help, she realized the stable area was empty. This time of day the thirty or so people who earned a living working for St. Vyr around the home ranch were probably inside resting from the burning heat of the day. The herders and farmers who normally would have been close by were doing the same in the orchards or out in the fields with the stock. Jeanne finished tying Redbird to the hitching rail and ran through the open doors on the courtyard to the house, shouting for her sisters, her grandmother and Margo the housekeeper.

"What is it, child?" Giselle, her grandmother asked in alarm when Jeanne burst through the French doors leading from the patio to the sitting room.

"Papa's tricorn came back without him," Jeanne gasped out. "There is blood on the stirrups, and he has a bullet burn across his rump. Where is everyone?"

"Margo went into town to do the weekly shopping," Bethany, her older sister said, referring to their housekeeper. "Did you say Papa was hurt? Where is he?"

"I don't know," Jeanne said. "Redbird was loose by the corral when I got back. At first, I didn't notice he was hurt. Where was Papa going today?"

"He went into town to see the lawyer," Iris, the next oldest sister, told her.

"Jeanne, go saddle us some mounts

while we change into riding clothes,"
Bethany ordered. Jeanne ran back outside.

Bethany looked at her grandmother, her
grey eyes worried. "Gran, You need to send
someone out to the men working in the
pastures closest to the house and have
them come in and help with the search. If
Papa was shot between the ranch and town,
he'll be found somewhere along the road to
the Crossing."

Giselle nodded her understanding and
left quickly, calling for Macon, the head
gardener.

Bethany came downstairs a few minutes
later, dressed in homespun grey pants and
shirt. The tight shirt and pants fit
snuggly on her hourglass figure, and the
grey color brought out the red highlights
in her hair. she went to her father's gun
cabinet and loaded rifles and pistols for
herself and her sisters. She belted on a
holster belt specially made to fit around
her waist. She slid a handgun into the
holster.

"Oh, no," Iris protested, her green
eyes widening when she saw the weapons.
She was tucking her white blond hair up
under a wide-brimmed leather hat. "Surely
we won't need those."

"If something happened to Papa,"
Bethany told Iris grimly, "It wasn't an
accident. Jeanne said Redbird had a bullet

burn across his rump. Do you want to be helpless if we need to rescue him?"

Bethany handed the second pistol and rifle to Iris who took it reluctantly. Despite her height, this middle girl of Michael St. Vyr's had an air of fragility, belied by the expertise with which she checked the pistol and rifle.

"Where is mine?" Giselle asked, returning from her errand. She and her granddaughters had changed to homespun pants, shirt and boots. She was a beautiful woman despite showing her fifty years of age and could still turn heads in the tight pants and shirt.

"In the gun cabinet because we need you need to stay here in case Papa makes it home," Jeanne informed her as she came back in through the window. She took her weapons from Bethany. "The Tricorns are ready to go."

"Thank you, Jeanne," Bethany said. She turned to Giselle. "You are our best doctor. You know you need to stay here in case someone brings Papa home wounded, Grandmother."

Giselle gave reluctant consent to the plan. "I'll give you girls three hours to find him before I'm coming out to look also."

The land between the Golden Tricorn and the town of River Crossing looked flat, but it was pocked with shallow dips and cuts in the Earth , making searching for a wounded man who might be trying to hide, slow and difficult work. The knee-high grass growing off the road could hide a body as well.

It was Iris who spotted the marks Michael had made when he dragged himself into the ditch for cover.

"Here!" Iris called, dismounting and sliding down into the waist deep ditch. Her tricorn smelled blood and pulled back nervously on the reins, nearly dragging her back up the embankment.

"Papa!" Jeanne called urgently. "Where are you?"

She too dismounted, and taking the reins of Iris's tricorn, she tied the nervous animal to her saddle horn. She had no fear of her own mount running off because she smelled blood; she had spent hours training Grayling not to flinch under more difficult circumstances than a smell she didn't care for. When Bethany dismounted, she handed the reins of the tricorns to her and joined Iris in the ditch, carefully lifting the bushes to see if her father had crawled under them.

Iris had just spotted one of Michael's boots sticking out from under a bush against the far bank, and she rushed forward, yanking the bushes out of her

way.

"Be careful. There might be a Sander under there. You know how they like the shade when it's hot," Bethany warned, referring to St. Antoni's large poisonous reptiles.

"So, shoot it with that damn gun you insisted we bring," Iris retorted, dropping beside her father and picking up his wrist to feel for a pulse.

Jeanne had finished moving the brush aside and she too dropped beside Michael. "He's bleeding. It looks as if someone shot him in the back. We need to get him out of here and back to the ranch."

"The doctor's house in town is closer," Bethany objected.

"Should we move him?" asked Iris doubtfully. "What if it hurts his back?"

"His back's already hurt," Jeanne snapped.

"That might not be relevant anyway," Bethany observed. "I don't think the three of us can get him back up the bank on our own. Here," she pulled bandages, rags and a bottle of alcohol out of her saddlebag. "One of you see if you can clean the wound and bandage it. I—"

Her head lifted sharply as she heard the unmistakable clop, clop of a buckboard driven by a team of tricorns coming down the road from town.

"It's Margo," she cried, waving frantically at the driver. Margo snapped the reins, and the team broke into a gallop, coming to a sliding stop when they reached the girls.

"What happened, Nina?" Margo asked.

"It's Papa. He's wounded, and he's down in the ditch. We will need help to get him out of there."

"Dios mio!" the middle-aged housekeeper exclaimed, tumbling off the wagon seat and coming to look down into the ditch.

"I think we'll soon have help to get him out of the ditch," Jeanne said, pointing to a plume of dust rising on the road from the direction of the ranch. Shortly, about fifteen of the ranch hands thundered up on lathered tricorns, demanding to know what had happened.

With their help, it proved easy to move the wounded man into Margo's buckboard. Margo made a wide, slow turn to jostle Michael as little as possible, and headed back into town. Iris and three of the hands, who were just aching for someone to attempt to stop them, rode with the wagon.

Bethany turned to Jeanne. "You'd better go back to the ranch and let Gran know what happened. She'll want to come into town. Take a couple of the men with you."

Jeanne nodded and remounted.

Bethany remounted her own tricorn and

looked over at the hands that had stayed with her. "Durango, who is the best tracker?" she asked a tall slim man with a wide brimmed hat.

"Red and I," he replied. "You want us to find out who did this?"

"Yes," she said grimly. "I'm putting you in charge. And Durango, when you find him, we need him alive to be able to talk to the Sheriff. I don't care if he dies afterward, just if he lives long enough to talk. I want to know who did this."

TO READ MORE: <u>CLICK HERE</u>

CPSIA information can be obtained
at www.ICGtesting.com
Printed in the USA
BVHW031022260321
603504BV00001B/12